Michael Underwood and The Murder Room

>>> This title is part of The Murder Room, our series dedicated to making available out-of-print or hard-to-find titles by classic crime writers.

Crime fiction has always held up a mirror to society. The Victorians were fascinated by sensational murder and the emerging science of detection; now we are obsessed with the forensic detail of violent death. And no other genre has so captivated and enthralled readers.

Vast troves of classic crime writing have for a long time been unavailable to all but the most dedicated frequenters of second-hand bookshops. The advent of digital publishing means that we are now able to bring you the backlists of a huge range of titles by classic and contemporary crime writers, some of which have been out of print for decades.

From the genteel amateur private eyes of the Golden Age and the femmes fatales of pulp fiction, to the morally ambiguous hard-boiled detectives of mid twentieth-century America and their descendants who walk our twenty-first century streets, The Murder Room has it all. **>>>**

The Murder Room
Where Criminal Minds Meet

themurderroom.com

T0351560

Michael Underwood (1916–1992)

Michael Underwood (the pseudonym of John Michael Evelyn) was born in Worthing, Sussex and educated at Christ Church College, Oxford. He was called to the Bar in 1939 and served in the British army during World War Two. He returned to work in the Department of Public Prosecutions until his retirement in 1976, and wrote almost 50 crime novels informed by his career in the law. His five series characters include Sergeant Nick Atwell and lawyer Rosa Epton, of whom is was said by the *Washington Post* that she 'outdoes Perry Mason'.

Murder on Trial

Michael Underwood

An Orion book

Copyright © Isobel Mackenzie 1954

The right of Michael Underwood to be identified as the author of this work has been asserted in accordance with the Copyright, Designs and Patents Act 1988.

This edition published by
The Orion Publishing Group Ltd
Orion House
5 Upper St Martin's Lane
London WC2H 9EA

An Hachette UK company
A CIP catalogue record for this book is available from the British Library

ISBN 978 1 4719 0764 7

www.orionbooks.co.uk

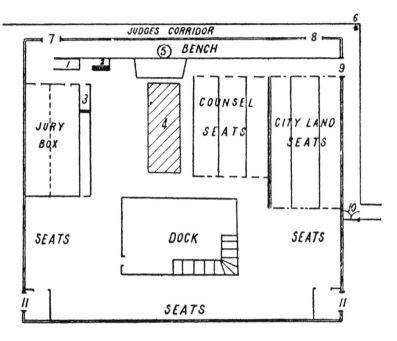

ROUGH DIAGRAM OF COURT NO. 1.

CENTRAL CRIMINAL COURT, OLD BAILEY,

LONDON, E.C.4

NOTE: Steps denoting the different floor levels are *not* marked.

Legend

1. Witness box
2. Shorthand-writer's desk
3. Court Inspector's seat
4. Table in well of Court
5. Judge
6. Judge's Usher's seat (in corridor outside Court)
7. Door leading to Judges' corridor, jury retiring rooms, etc.

8. Door by which Judge enters
9. Door by which users of City Lands seats enter
10. Swing doors dividing public and private parts of the building
11. Two main entrances for jurors, witnesses, etc.

Chapter One

'Do you think I shall be all right in my dark blue suit?'
Mr. Pinty asked his wife.

They were having breakfast and Mrs. Pinty was at
that moment more interested in her paper than her husband's dark blue suit. Seeing to his breakfast and
snatching some for herself before starting on the daily
housewife's round usually gave her no time for looking
at newspapers. Only those with cooks and parlourmaids
and no shopping problems could enjoy that breakfast
luxury. But on this particular morning, there was a
break in routine and Mr. Pinty wasn't leaving the house
until half an hour after his usual time. So it was that
Mrs. Pinty, waiting for him to come down to his plate
of porridge and two dubious-looking sausages, had
picked up the *Morning Echo* and soon become engrossed
in an intimate account of the love life of an Eastern
potentate who had apparently left five wives in Asia to
come and plight his oriental troth with a Midland
beauty queen whose picture had somehow found its way
into one of his palaces. The picture hadn't shown, and
the roving-eyed potentate wasn't to know, that the lady
had chronic adenoids and was the only contestant.

'It's awfully shiny at the elbows', continued Mr.
Pinty. His wife sighed and tore her gaze from the paper.

'It's your best and I don't see that anyone is going to
look at your elbows.' This was a more than reasonable
reply when none was really required.

It was about a week before that John Pinty had

received a summons to attend the Central Criminal Court as a juror. Since then he had lived in a gentle hum of excitement and his wife had several times reflected that a summons from the Archangel Gabriel himself could not have given him more to fuss about. There was absolutely no doubt that he glowed with righteous pride at the prospect of his forthcoming duties, and Mrs. Pinty had on several evenings had to listen to disquisitions on the rights and privileges of citizenship in a parliamentary democracy.

John Pinty was middle-aged, and stood about five foot six inches in his socks. He wore thick-lens spectacles with austere gold rims and he parted his hair which was dark, carefully in the middle, the two front bits on each side of the parting giving the appearance of tidy bay windows. What he had, he had fought for. He had no social background and no inherited wealth, but he had been the faithful servant of the same firm for over twenty-five years and now (he had recently attained his two score years and ten) he owned a modest but pleasant house in one of the many new roads out Edgware way. He also had a television set and a 1937 Austin 10 which knew the Southend road by heart. Malcolm, who was fourteen, was doing well at a nearby Grammar School, and Cynthia, who was five years older, was training to be a nurse, but looked like getting married long before that aim was achieved.

At the office Mr. Pinty had not referred to his coming jury duties after the first day, when much to his annoyance young Barnes, the new junior clerk, had shown him up as not knowing that the Central Criminal Court was the correct name of the building more commonly called the Old Bailey.

2

Later he had gone in to see Mr. Packer who was the partner who dealt with staff matters, to ask him about taking time off. Mr. Pinty had been considerably exercised in his own mind about whether to ask Mr. Packer if this would be all right or whether simply to tell him politely that he wouldn't be in the office that day as Her Majesty required him on other business. In the end he had decided that it would be more prudent to approach Mr. Packer as senior clerk in Ripson, Morley, Packer and Co., than as a privileged citizen now summoned to try the several issues joined between his Sovereign Lady the Queen and the prisoner at the bar.

'Good morning, Mr. Packer.'

Mr. Packer looked up from his desk and nodded.

'Good morning, Pinty, what can I do for you?'

'Mr. Packer, I've had a summons to serve as a juror at the Old Bailey next week. Will it be in order for me to be away from the office?'

Mr. Packer smiled. 'You'll have to pay a whacking great fine if you don't turn up there.'

This was not of course strictly true, but Mr. Packer could never resist making gentle jabs at Mr. Pinty's slight suburban pomposity. The former had known security all his life but it was the latter who would fight to his last breath to keep the little security with which he had so diligently walled himself about. Mr. Packer continued:

'I was on a jury just before the war. For three days we sat about in draughty corridors and grew corns on our backsides, and then for the next three we tried a dreary commonplace little man' (not unlike you, Pinty, he'd almost said) 'who'd defrauded his mother-

3

in-law of her Post-Office savings. She was a grim looking old bird and so we added a recommendation to mercy and the chap only got six months.'

Mr. Pinty smiled, not because he was particularly amused, but because Mr. Packer was a partner; and a clerk, albeit the senior one, is always respectful to partners; for after all he knew his hard-won security was not impregnable.

And now the great day had arrived and Mr. Pinty had put on his best suit and was fussing about his shiny elbows. For that matter the carpet was worn too, and the chair covers were so faded that the pattern was no longer discernible. With prices what they are, you couldn't have everything new on £500 a year. But Mrs. Pinty, who was really very fond of her husband, forbore to point this out. Theirs was a contented and uneventful life, but she sometimes looked at him and reflected how little she really knew him. She supposed it would always be so, and that there were probably hundreds and thousands of other ordinary wives who felt the same way about their ordinary husbands. She felt it was probably largely her fault in that she had always accepted his face value and never made any effort to pry into his mind or his background. He had proposed to her over his shoulder on a tandem ride, she had accepted him and they had then ridden on for another two miles before dismounting and having their sandwiches. This unromantic start had set the tenor to their whole married life.

'Do you know what case you'll be on? Isn't that Tarrant murder starting to-day?'

Mr. Pinty looked momentarily startled.

'I'm not sure I'd like a murder case—but I suppose

it's better than someone who has defrauded his mother-in-law', he said, recalling Mr. Packer's experiences.

His wife helped him into his greatcoat, handed him his gloves and watched him step out into the gloom of a November morning. But Mr. Pinty didn't notice the cold, and Mr. Packer, had he been there, would hardly have recognized his senior clerk. He hadn't exactly changed physically overnight, but there was a thoughtful smile about his mouth which wasn't usually there. Yes, it would be interesting if he was one of the jurors in the Tarrant trial—very interesting in fact, mused Mr. Pinty.

A ten-minute walk brought him to the tube station where he became anonymous in a jostling crowd of hundreds of other Mr. Pintys, all bound for their offices and a day of unremitting routine toil midst the files and ledgers which help to make the business world go round.

Chapter Two

MR. PINTY arrived at the Old Bailey much too early and, after first being told that the queue for the public gallery was outside and round the corner, was directed to sit on a hard seat in a draughty corridor outside the Court. Having left his paper in the tube, he had nothing to do but survey his surroundings.

After a time, various people started to move up and down the corridor. Important looking barristers wearing preoccupied looks mounted the stairs and disappeared from view only to return shortly after disguised in wig and gown. Mr. Pinty amused himself seeing whether he was able to recognize them again when they reappeared after exchanging bowler hats for wigs.

A pale-faced young woman sat down beside him. She wore a shabby coat over a cheap cotton dress and the cold added to the pinched look of anxiety on her face. With her was a small girl who snivelled continuously and who had successfully covered her face with crumbs from the unappetizing-looking rock bun which she desperately clutched in one of her dirty little hands. Mr. Pinty was just reflecting that she was hardly proper company for a juror when the woman turned to him and spoke in a harsh bitter voice.

'Joe's going to get a packet from that old bastard this morning and it weren't his fault.'

Mr. Pinty was so flustered by this observation that he could think of nothing more suitable to say than a polite, 'Oh—really?'

'Yes, there ain't no justice in this ruddy building. And what do they think *I'm* going to do with Joe inside?'

By this time the benches, where they were sitting, were full and Mr. Pinty's anxious glances for alternative accommodation only confirmed his inescapable plight.

'What you up 'ere for?' went on the woman, oblivious of Mr. Pinty's embarrassment.

'I'm a juror.'

This announcement brought him a look of such contemptuous distaste that he was infinitely relieved when, at that moment, a tall thin policeman shouted out: 'Jurors Number One Court, this way please.'

Mr. Pinty positively leapt from his seat and was first to reach the officer. The latter led them into Court and told them to sit in some seats at the back of the dock. This time, he found himself sitting next to a middle-aged female who looked rather like a South American parrot. She was dressed in bright forest green, and brightly coloured feathers adorned her felt hat. She had a pair of gold-rimmed lorgnettes which were in constant use as she scrutinized the increased comings and goings in the Court. She turned to Mr. Pinty and in a rich hoarse voice spoke to him.

'I hear we're going to try the Tarrant case—you know, the man who shot that poor young policeman.'

'Oh yes?' replied Mr. Pinty, trying to sound both interested and intelligent.

By now, the Court was filling up. The public gallery, high up on the right, had been packed as soon as the doors opened. In the seats beneath it sat smartly-dressed women and their prosperous-looking male escorts. Young barristers in very white wigs came in in pairs and tried to look as if they'd snatched time from their own busy practices to come and lend a hand.

Mr. Pinty's companion was about to speak to him again when the Clerk of the Court, a rather lugubrious-looking man, who wore pince-nez and had a deep but gloomy voice called out, 'Will the members of the jury in waiting please come into the jury box as I call out their names.'

He picked a card from the wooden box in front of him. 'Mr. John Pinty. Is Mr. Pinty there?' he asked petulantly when there was no immediate response. He was, but was so startled at being called first he hadn't moved. It was the first time he had ever been ahead of his fellow creatures in anything since at the age of eight he was given a prize for good attendance at Sunday School.

Five others then trooped after him and together they filled the front row of the jury box.

'Miss Eugenie Victoria Fenwick-Blunt', called the clerk, and the parrot woman came into the box and sat down in the second row directly behind Mr. Pinty, who was now tormented by the recollection that it was usually the juror in his seat who acted as foreman. He was almost sure that it was always the person who sat nearest the judge in the front row and that was certainly where he was now sitting. By this time everyone was in his place. Besides Miss Fenwick-Blunt there was only one other woman on the jury. She was a pretty girl who was in the back row to the obvious delight of the young man who sat next to her. An unusual place for a budding romance but, after all, love recognizes no limits and an impish cupid might rightly class it as one of his better efforts to make a match between two jurors in a murder trial.

Just below Mr. Pinty in a little box by himself sat Inspector Robert MacBruce. With two rows of medals on his chest and a massive frame, he looked as if he were planted in his seat for life. MacBruce was a dour Scot who had come to London as a young man and joined the Metropolitan Force. He was not particularly popular either with his brother inspectors or with those who had to serve under him. As he sat waiting for the judge to come in, he recalled the first (and last) time he had met William Edgar Tarrant. No, he for one was not sorry to see him on trial for murder, and if, as was generally expected, Tarrant was convicted, then equally MacBruce would not be amongst his mourners on the day of his execution.

But, like everyone else, MacBruce was surprised that Tarrant had landed himself in murder. That wasn't his line of country at all. In his several earlier exploits, which had resulted in the police laying a heavy hand on his shoulder, he had never been known to carry arms. It was with silvery cultured words and an old school tie that he separated women with more money than sense from their possessions, not with a revolver. It was all done charmingly over a cocktail at Lady Mink's; during the first interval of *Aida* at Covent Garden; or once during the final set of the men's singles at Wimbledon. The victims on many occasions had been quite annoyed at the inartistic intervention of the police, and many months after when Tarrant was once more locked up, they had sighed with the pleasurable memory of it all.

The Inspector cast his gaze along the two back rows

9

of seats behind counsel (where Mr. Pinty had seen the smart folk go) and reflected that several of the fashionable women who sat there would still probably grasp the chance of being cheated so enchantingly if they could have it. Thus went MacBruce's thoughts on this November morning as he sat waiting in his little box. The girl who had just come in with the rather ordinary looking man, attracted his eye. She looked fresh and pretty and the Inspector idly wondered who she was.

Thank heavens she's come at last, thought Jakes Hartman, the shorthand writer, as he sat in his little box beneath the witness box and watched her sit down and look around. Jakes had first seen Maisie Jenks at a tennis club dance a few weeks before, where she had been the bored member of a large party which her slightly older brother Ronald had got up. Jakes had taken an immediate liking to Maisie whom he'd met by cheating in a Paul Jones, and at the same time a strong dislike to her brother Ronald whom he regarded as a young rip. In this judgment he wasn't far wrong, as Ronald Jenks was one of those young men who thought highly of themselves and caused their parents considerable anxiety by their complete lack of stability. Before the dance was over Jakes knew he was in love with Maisie, but since then progress had been slow and thus he had leapt at the chance of doing her this favour.

She had mentioned that she and her father particularly wanted to get in to the Tarrant trial as she had known him very slightly in the past. Jakes understood that Tarrant had once made a vague pass at her, and she couldn't stand him, and he, Jakes, was content to see him swing for this reason alone. They had always wanted to attend a murder trial, and it made it undeniably more interesting if you knew something of the person concerned.

Accordingly Jakes had been delighted when Maisie asked him if he could get them into Court, and had immediately said that of course he could. He had then set about wondering how to do it, and felt it was essential to his reputation they should sit in the best seats. Finally it had all been arranged and he had phoned Maisie to tell her what time to arrive and to be sure not to be late. And now here she and her father were arriving only a moment or so before the judge took his seat, and at least a quarter of an hour after he had told them to be there. Still, Maisie looked adorable. She had on a pale blue coat and hat which went well with her curly fair hair and fresh complexion—or so Jakes Hartman thought. But then his state was such that he would probably have thought she looked equally attractive in gym kit and a straw boater. He glanced at Mr. Jenks and was surprised that he had such an attractive daughter. He was of less than average height, had dark hair parted in the middle and was in fact a very ordinary looking little man. This was the first time that Jakes had seen him although Maisie had once or twice vaguely said that she must introduce him.

Having settled herself in her seat, Maisie gazed around the Court. To Jakes, sitting at his funny little desk between the Clerk of the Court and the witness box, she flashed a friendly smile. Directly opposite to where she was sitting was the jury box, now filled with twelve slightly nervous people. Certainly the poor little man with the thick gold-rimmed spectacles, who was sitting in the foreman's seat, looked thoroughly ill at ease. Immediately in front of the jury box Maisie noted

11

the cramped but crowded press box and on the far right of them in his little cubby hole beneath the foreman sat Inspector MacBruce. All that separated him from Jakes Hartman were the four narrow steps which led up to the witness box.

At the big table in the well of the Court sat several men who were busy turning the leaves of files, or sorting out documents which were piled before them. These were the police officers and solicitors, and the table at which they sat stretched from the Clerk of the Court's desk to within two feet of the gigantic dock which completely filled the centre of the Court. Behind it were some tiered seats which were now packed with people who'd managed to gain admittance to the court.

The row of seats between where Maisie and her father were sitting and the big solid table in the well of the Court were filled with bewigged barristers. Over Maisie's head projected the public gallery. Those in its front row had been queueing since the early hours of the morning, and they now gazed down upon the animated scene below: the great empty dock and the line of big heavy leather chairs which faced it and in one of which the Judge would shortly be taking his seat. Behind the centre seat, the City sword glistened against the wall. All this, Maisie's eye took in as she gazed about her. She was sorry that the barristers had their backs to her and that she was unable to study their faces.

Mr. Pinty, however, from his seat in the front row of the jury could and did study them. The one on the left of the front row, whom he presumed was for the prosecution, was a short spare man with very blue eyes and a nice smile. The one at the other end was the complete opposite. He was large and bulky, and he had a red face which in repose looked particularly unintelligent. His wig was dirty and the curls looked as though they might drop off if he shook his head. From time to time he dropped his spectacles to the end of his nose and spoke in a very audible whisper to the earnest young man next to him who was his junior in the case. One of his comments to the effect that the jury looked a 'pretty average stupid bunch' was almost sufficient to convict Tarrant before he ever got into the dock.

Jakes Hartman had listened to Alan Sands, the prosecuting counsel who held the appointment of first Senior Treasury Counsel at the Central Criminal Court, in innumerable murder cases. He was calm and logical, had a clear voice and never said an unnecessary word. For these last two attributes Jakes held him in great esteem. Not so, old Sir Genser Fakeleigh Q.C. (widely known as the Old Fake amongst the younger members of the profession). He boomed and boomed, and it usually all added up to nothing. But it all had to be written down, reflected Jakes grimly. He was ponderous only to give birth to the ripest platitudes of the day and he had the pomposity of a penguin. In fact, the only difference between them was that penguins were not given to platitudes, and the Old Fake didn't lay eggs, so far as was known.

Outside in the corridor behind the bench, Alfred Knight, the Judge's Usher, rapped sharply four times on the door and threw it open. Everyone stood up. An under-sheriff followed by two aldermen in blue robes entered and bowed to Mr. Justice Blaney as he passed between them and took his seat. Mr. Justice Blaney was a very ordinary judge, if one may use that epithet in respect of any of Her Majesty's judges. He had none of the little habits or quirks which are so often associated with, and indeed expected of, judges. He had no mannerisms and was completely free of pedantry. He had a slightly dry sense of humour and most Counsel enjoyed appearing before him. Although a very ordinary judge, he was far from being an undistinguished one.

After an usher had intoned in a meaningless voice something about 'My Lords, the Queen's Justices', everyone sat down.

'Put up William Edgar Tarrant', said the clerk, and into the dock stepped a man of about forty. He had black hair which was well greased and neatly parted. His features were regular but lacked strength in the whole, and there was now a certain pouchiness beneath the eyes. It was the confident tread of self-assurance that brought Tarrant to the front of the dock, where he was at once conscious of all eyes upon him. The eyes of Judge and Counsel which coolly appraised him and others which tried to look into his very soul to see what thoughts a murderer harboured there.

'Not guilty', he replied to the clerk, a moment later.

Of course he hadn't murdered P.C. Daniel Moss on the night of the eleventh September last, but it now looked as if it was going to be a formidable task to persuade a jury of the fact. The Crown had assembled a strong case of circumstantial evidence against him. Before the day was out he would know exactly what he had got to face. He hoped it would not be necessary to bring in others, but if things went badly for him, then he would have to. After all, it was his life which was at stake, and honour must know some limits. As it was, he was quite surprised at the loyalty he had already shown a fellow-thief.

The jury were now being sworn and Tarrant watched them casually, not that he was likely to want to object to any of them. It amused him to see how practically each of them stumbled over the oath and even the apparently educated ones seemed unable to read simple English. As for the first little man, he might have been doing an ill-learned recitation at a school concert. True enough, Mr. Pinty had made a fearful mess over it, but he was now sitting back and listening with considerable relief to his colleagues who were little better. People in court had smiled when the parrot female behind him attempted to hold the testament and her lorgnettes in the same hand, with the result that she dropped the former and was tersely told by the usher to start all over again. They really were rather like a lot of nervous children and the usher, who had known juries for more years than he cared to recall, was an uncompromising taskmaster. These twelve men and women on whom Tarrant's future, indeed his very life, depended, were at that moment quite the most uncomfortable and self-conscious little band of people in London. The irony of the situation was not lost on Tarrant, who above all else was a man of the world, and furthermore one who had previously had first-hand opportunities of observing the ways of juries from the self-same position which he now occupied.

'Sit now.'

It was the warder Albert Glindy who accompanied the remark with a nudge, and Tarrant sat down. He and Glindy had seen a lot of each other recently, the latter being one of his constant companions and a warder at the prison where he'd been awaiting trial.

Alan Sands was on his feet now.

'May it please your Lordship, members of the jury, in this case I appear for the Crown with my learned friend Mr. Beech, and the prisoner has the advantage of being defended by my learned friends Sir Genser Fakeleigh and Mr. Grange.'

How the law loves its little formulæ, thought Tarrant, who also had several doubts about the advantage of being defended by Sir Genser. Alan Sands went on:

'On the evening of the eleventh of September, Police Constable Moss was on duty in the Abbey Hill district of north west London, when he noticed two men behaving suspiciously near one of the large houses which abound in that part. He watched them for some time and eventually he must have gone up to them to ask them their business. . . . He was immediately shot through the stomach by one of the men and . . . both ran off with the blasts of the dying constable's whistle ringing in their ears . . . ' Yes, that was true enough and Tarrant relived the scene for a few moments. '. . . envelope found nearby obviously dropped by one of the men as he fled. It was addressed to the prisoner and on the back was drawn a rough sketch which is easily identifiable as this particular part of Abbey Hill . . . evidence of a taxi-driver who picked up a man who the Crown say is the prisoner, near Abbey Hill tube station just after midnight . . . murder committed eleven forty-five . . . This man was out of breath and had obviously been running . . . prisoner arrested three days later in South London where he was lodging under a false name . . .'

And so the story was unfolded in simple undramatic language, and after a time Tarrant ceased to listen to it, but instead grimly reflected that it was certainly the toughest spot he had yet been in. There was only one possible way out; only one loophole through which he could escape and that was to tell not only the truth but the whole truth. It would need cool thought and a firm decision though. But he found it difficult to concentrate on his desperate plight and he had little faith in Sir Genser's ability to extricate him. Fortunately he was unaware that the former had already antagonized the jury by his loud and tactless aside. It would be up to him to save himself and it wasn't a job which could be entrusted to his legal representatives.

He looked at Inspector MacBruce who was yawning and wondered if he still felt sore at what had happened when they last saw each other twelve years ago. He imagined that he probably did, but after all it was his own fault. He gazed up at the public gallery and then at the seats beneath it. He wondered who the man was who was staring at him so intently. The girl next to him was rather pretty and her face seemed vaguely familiar. She now seemed very much interested in one of the jurors.

Alan Sands had finished his opening speech and now witnesses were going into the box. First a draughtsman produced a plan and then a photographer produced an album of photographs, some of them harmless but one or two rather gruesome ones which made the pretty girl on the jury involuntarily shrink away. There was really nothing for Tarrant's Counsel to ask these witnesses, but silence was not Sir Genser's strong point.

'Tell me, officer, is the lamp-post in the first photograph the same one as that shown in the second?'

'Yes, sir', said the officer civilly, and Judge and

17

jury looked at the lamp-post with fresh interest only to realize the complete fatuity of the question.

'Thank you, officer. That's all I wish to put to this witness, m'lord', boomed Sir Genser, and sank down to his seat again with a look of triumph.

Occasionally Tarrant listened attentively to bits of the evidence, but he knew what the witnesses were going to say anyway and he had more important things on his mind. The sands of time were fast running out and soon he would have to make an irrevocable decision. He looked across at the Judge who had hardly spoken a word since the case began. Having a sense of history, he recalled that in this same court down the ages, England's most illustrious judges had sat and faced her most notorious criminals, and that each had bowed to their country's most ordinary citizens who assembled there to give the vital decision.

And so the day wore on and eventually came to a close. The jury had settled down and by now felt quite old hands at the game. Jakes Hartman thought to himself, thank heavens it's almost time to adjourn; and Maisie muttered to her father that the glamour had worn off and she'd sooner read Edgar Wallace any day.

In answer to a query from the Judge, Sir Genser replied that the prisoner was the only witness he would call.

'He will go into the box and tell his story to-morrow morning, m'lord.'

Mr. Justice Blaney got up and everyone else in Court rose to their feet also. The aged usher was about to intone his final piece for the day when Tarrant spoke first.

'I'd like to say, my lord, that when I give my evidence

to-morrow, I shall be forced to make certain disclosures.'

The warders each side of him closed in and hissed: 'Quiet', as all eyes in Court were riveted on him. But he had finished almost before they realized what he had said. The die was now cast.

Chapter Three

'WONDER what he's going to say', Detective Chief Inspector Simon Manton said to his companion, Detective Sergeant Andrew Talper, as they gathered their papers together.

'Don't see there's much he can say', replied the other.

'Oh he's got something on his mind all right and he's going to spill it. Ah, well, we'll have to wait till tomorrow. You know, Andy, I've always felt there was something queer about this case ever since we started on it. I know it seems a simple enough one on the surface, but . . . Bad luck his being defended by the Old Fake; not that it can make any difference.'

The court was deserted as Manton and Sergeant Talper picked up the last of their belongings and went out. It was just an empty room again. With its last occupants went the drama which had permeated its atmosphere during the day.

Manton and Talper left the building and drove back to the Yard. This was the fourth murder case they had worked on together and each one had been successful, so that they had got themselves quite a reputation, not only with the sensation-seeking public, but also with their tougher and more cynical colleagues.

Simon Manton was, at thirty-six, the youngest Detective Chief Inspector at the Yard. He had been destined for the Army, but when family fortunes crumbled just as he was about to go to Sandhurst, he went to London and joined the Metropolitan Police.

From a P.C. on the beat he had mounted the ladder by sheer hard work, and now he was not only respected, but well liked, by both his junior and his senior officers, and that in spite of the fact that he was a 'college boy'. He had the trim figure of an athlete and though his fair hair was getting thin in front, he certainly didn't look older than his years. He had striking blue eyes and a friendly smile which revealed perfect teeth. Like most senior detectives in the Metropolitan Police Force he was always perfectly dressed. Sergeant Talper was some four years his senior in age. He came of a large west-country family and now had a fair-sized one himself. He had the face of a friendly tough and a far sharper mind than his looks portrayed. He was never averse to a bit of rough and tumble, not that there was ever much of that sort of thing in a murder case. He enjoyed working with Manton and had a great and loyal admiration for him.

When her husband got home that evening, Mrs. Pinty expected to be regaled with a long account of his experiences, but in fact he was extremely uncommunicative and almost brusque when she asked him how things had gone.

'The Judge told us not to discuss the case with anyone, dear. You can read about it in the evening paper,' he added as an after-thought.

'You haven't even told me what case it is', said Mrs. Pinty, nettled by his tone.

'Oh, it's the Tarrant murder case, and there's a long account in the *Evening Echo*.'

'I'm quite sure he didn't mean you couldn't even discuss it with your own wife.'

But this only got an even shorter reply.

'I'm quite sure he did.'

'Well, thank heavens you're not a juror every day, is all I can say', said Mrs. Pinty, who by now felt both vexed and slighted.

After this, Mr. Pinty quickly changed the subject but only finally succeeded in thawing his wife shortly before they retired for the night.

Jakes Hartman had not had an opportunity of speaking to Maisie all day. He had expected that she and her father would wait outside the Court at the end of the day's proceedings, to have a word with him. But they hadn't been there and on inquiring, he had been told by the police officer at the door that they had gone straight downstairs and not hung about at all. Jakes was, not unnaturally perhaps, a bit peeved, and decided that Maisie should know it too.

When he telephoned her that night after supper, it was her brother Ronnie who answered. This didn't help to soothe him either, and he reflected again on the mystery of genetics which provided an adorable girl with such an ordinary looking father and odious young brother.

'Is Miss Maisie Jenks in?'

'Yes. Do you want to speak to her?'

'Please', said Jakes, reflecting how much he disliked phoning his girl-friends. He never managed to get through to them straight away. Sometimes it was kid brothers or married sisters who picked up the receiver: at others it was garrulous mothers or fed-up fathers whose voices came down the line. On all occasions Jakes felt at a disadvantage, and he always got the impression that the person at the other end knew all about him, while he knew little of them. It was most unfair.

A muffled shout of: 'Maisie, some bloke wants you on the phone', broke in on his uneasy thoughts. He heard a brisk click of heels getting nearer and then Maisie's voice.

'Hello, is that you, Jakes?'

'Yes, it is, but how on earth did you know? I'm not the only person who phones you, am I?'

His heart would have jumped for joy if he could have got an affirmative answer to this, but he hardly expected one and so wasn't disappointed when Maisie went on: 'No, you're not—but I was expecting you to ring up. I feel I owe you an apology about this afternoon. I mean about leaving without having a word with you.'

'Oh, that's all right', he said handsomely.

'Well, it was really Daddy's fault. He wanted to dash off. It was all rather fun, wasn't it?'

Jakes' experience was that people generally selected rather inappropriate expressions to describe a murder trial.

'What a priceless old boy that is who is defending Tarrant; and the one who is prosecuting isn't a bit like I imagined he would be.'

'Why, what did you expect then?'

'Well not that anyway. I thought he'd wave his arms about more and . . .'

'He's not Sir Thomas Beecham!'

It occurred to Jakes that so far he'd said nothing to indicate to Maisie that he thought her conduct worthy of censure; but after all she had apologized after a fashion and he didn't wish to do anything irreparable.

'Can we come again to-morrow? Daddy says he'd

like to see the end of the trial. Of course we were both awfully impressed by you in your little corner.'

'I bet you were; but when am I going to see you again? I mean see you properly and not just look at you across the Court. What about a movie to-morrow evening?'

'Yes, I'd like that, Jakes. Will you come and call for me? You must meet Daddy sometime—he wants to meet you—but he's so often out in the evenings. He is to-night.'

Jakes felt much restored by this conversation and finished it off with a fresh protestation of his love for her.

Emerging from the stale cigarette smell of the call-box, he went into the nearest pub and had a pint of beer before going home.

As he lay sleepless in his cell that night, Tarrant rehearsed in his mind just how he would tell his story in the witness box the next day. He had really known all along that he would have to take the course which he had now decided on. The case against him was too strong for it to be otherwise. He was sorry though, that it had turned out that way; but no one could say he hadn't warned them. He reflected how his solicitor had several times told him that it was most important that he kept nothing back from him. Nevertheless he was glad that he hadn't followed this excellent advice and had reserved to himself the ultimate decision of how much he would say in the witness box. This was a case where he must be the judge in his own cause. So pondering, he dropped off to sleep.

Chapter Four

THE next day was foggy. Not so thick that one felt one was in a tureen full of soup, but sufficient to dislocate trains and buses and make everyone arrive at their work late and feeling irritable.

The fog had penetrated into Number One Court at the Old Bailey, and it left a dirty taste in the mouth. Inspector Manton and Detective Sergeant Talper were there early. The former reflected that his part in the case was now finished and that Tarrant's fate was in the hands of Judge, jury and maybe Home Secretary. Inspector MacBruce came over to him as he sat at the large heavy table in the well of the Court.

'Any idea what he's going to say this morning?' asked the uniformed Inspector.

'Who, Tarrant?'

'Yes, there's no chance of his springing some surprise and getting away with it, is there?'

'Not as far as I know, but there are one or two odd features about the case and I'm certain he's got something on his mind. However, we'll soon know what it's all about.'

MacBruce frowned. It struck him that Manton didn't seem as worried about the matter as he ought to be. It was his job to get inside the murderer's mind and know what he was thinking, not sit back and apparently adopt a wait-and-see attitude. Anyway, MacBruce had always thought the C.I.D. were overrated. They were glamour boys who rushed around in chauffeur-driven cars and got their pictures in the paper, leaving the victim's house or gazing into a pond which was being dragged. The truth was, of course, that Manton had done his job and it was now up to others; and he was never one to fidget and fuss about the result of one of his cases, provided his mind was clear that for his part he had left nothing undone. But the uniformed inspector was a persistent Scot.

'Then you've no idea what he meant when he spoke from the dock last night?'

'No, none', said Manton blandly.

MacBruce turned away sharply and walked back to his official seat and Manton gave Sergeant Talper an amused wink.

It was just before half-past ten and the Court was almost full again. Those up in the public gallery either read their newspapers or craned forward to watch every movement below. To them it was rather like a theatre as the orchestra come in one by one and start tuning their instruments.

The lugubrious-looking clerk called out the names of the jurors. They were all there except the woman who sat immediately behind Mr. Pinty. Her name was shouted in the corridors outside and she hurried into Court out of breath and more parrot-like than ever, her lorgnettes tossing wildly on her bosom as she made her way to the jury box.

Sir Genser Fakeleigh was sharpening the coloured pencils with which he underlined everything with such vigour and abandon that he often obliterated whole sentences. But the sight was an impressive one as he grasped them in one hand and with an air of great concentration made sweeping strokes with the other. Even if the jury weren't always impressed, his client invariably was.

Miss Fenwick-Blunt, having regained her composure and recovered her breath, leant forward to speak to Mr. Pinty.

'You've got a dreadful cold this morning.'

This was only too obvious, as Mr. Pinty was incessantly mopping his nose and inhaling eucalyptus vapour from his large white handkerchief.

Jakes Hartman gazed at the jury with the contemptuous eye of a drill-sergeant looking over a bunch of new recruits. He had little doubt that they would make the usual heavy weather at arriving at their verdict and from the look of one or two of them, anything might happen. There wasn't one you'd look at twice in the street, except perhaps the two women and at them for quite different reasons. The male jurors looked an unusually ordinary and uninspired selection: just about as ordinary as Maisie's father, in fact, reflected Jakes without malice.

An air of expectancy prevailed in Court. Tarrant's remark of the previous evening had brought the press along in even greater strength than on the first day. He'd always been a wonderful subject for them to write about, and now it looked as though he was going out in a blaze of dramatic glory. The murmur of conversation ceased abruptly as four raps on the door from the unseen Alfred Knight in the corridor outside brought everyone to their feet, and Mr. Justice Blaney walked slowly to his seat on the bench and stood waiting for the usher to finish his piece of recitation. Then he bowed to the City dignitaries who had entered with him, to the jury and to Counsel and sat down.

'Put up Tarrant', said the clerk, and all eyes turned to the large dock.

For a few moments no one appeared at all and the dock looked even larger in its emptiness. Eyes turned expectantly towards the Judge but Mr. Justice Blaney sat patiently looking at the back of the Court.

'It's quite incredible the way that just as the Judge takes his seat they always let them go to the W.C.', Alan Sands whispered to his junior.

A rumbling of footsteps from below heralded Tarrant's arrival. As he mounted the steep and narrow staircase which leads from the cells into the dock, he looked about him. On the third step from the top he could just see over the edge of the dock and his gaze met twelve pairs of curious eyes—the eyes of his judges, the eyes of ordinary, very ordinary citizens who were in due course going to decide whether he should continue his life or not. He reached the top and quite slowly and deliberately made his short way to the front, conscious of being the centre of everyone's interest, conscious too that Glindy was impatiently trying to hurry him. But Tarrant was not to be hurried. This might be his last appearance in public. When he left the dock, it might be to descend into oblivion where never again would he see his fellow creatures, where never again would he be seen as an ordinary man but only as a name and set of facts to the Home Secretary, and a height and a weight to the executioner. Anyway Glindy was the last person he'd allow to treat him in any summary fashion. He half turned his head and said something barely audible over his shoulder. For one brief moment Albert Glindy, Warder in H.M. Prison Service, looked like a dog that had been unexpectedly whipped; but then his pale, pointed face became impassive again.

Tarrant was dressed as on the previous day and he was as well groomed as if he were going to an Embassy party instead of into the witness box to fight for his life. With a courteous little nod to the Court in general, a sort of recognition for their attention, he pulled up his trouser legs and sat down.

Sir Genser Fakeleigh hoisted himself to his feet.

'I'll call my client immediately, m'lord.'

'Just before you do that Sir Genser, I want the short-hand writer to read back part of the evidence we heard yesterday.'

The Judge looked down over his desk at Jakes whose attention had been momentarily distracted by the two rather elegant young men who, he noted with annoyance, were sitting on either side of Maisie. He presumed that her father must have got held up by the fog, but he nevertheless reflected savagely on some people's unpunctual ways which resulted in their daughters being exposed to competitive masculine wiles. Almost needless to say, there was not the slightest justification for Jakes' searing thoughts but he was in fact so besotted where Maisie was concerned that Mr. Justice Blaney had to speak a trifle louder.

'Mr. Shorthand-writer, will you please read back to me the last answer given by Inspector Manton when he was under cross-examination yesterday afternoon. I think Sir Genser asked him if he had any idea who the man was, who the Crown alleged was with the accused on the night of the crime?'

Jakes flicked back through his notebook and stood up to answer the Judge.

'Yes, my lord, Inspector Manton said: "So far our inquiries in this connection have not borne fruit but they are continuing, and it is hoped——" '

'Thank you. Yes, Sir Genser, you're now going to put your client into the box, is that right?'

Sir Genser turned towards the dock.

'Go into the witness box, Tarrant, would you?'

Again all eyes turned on the prisoner who calmly got up, straightened his tie and then turned about, to walk to the door at the back of the dock—the door to freedom. Would he leave the Court by that door? Or would his last exit be down those steep steps until he disappeared from the view of the curious eyes whose only further interest in him would be satisfied in the Sunday newspapers?

In fact it was to be neither.

Tarrant stepped from the dock closely followed by Glindy. This was his moment, and always possessing a sense of the dramatic, it was one that was not lost on him. He moved down the two steps and between the press box and the backs of the chairs at the big table in the well of the Court where Inspector Manton and Detective Sergeant Talper were sitting. He looked up at the witness box which lay ahead, a small wooden rostrum from which so many lives had been sworn away in the past, and whose wooden top had resounded with legion desperate lies in attempts to save those lives. As he got level with the end of the big table, he turned left to mount the four steps which would bring him to that fatal stand where so many had stood and quailed.

But that was as near to it as he was ever to get; for at that moment a chilling scream shattered the atmosphere and Maisie Jenks collapsed in a dead faint. Before anyone could speak, there was a loud explosion and Tarrant quite gracefully crumpled at the knees and fell face down shot through the heart.

Chapter Five

THE general effect in Court was as if bombs were falling. Those who still had a few senses left, ducked, and those who hadn't, clutched their neighbours and screamed.

It was surprising, however, how quickly comparative order was once more restored. Sir Genser had to be assisted up, having got all but firmly wedged beneath Counsel's bench, and Manton's chair was rendered immovable by the prostrate body of Tarrant which lay on the floor directly behind it.

The first person to say anything of any consequence was the Judge who had neither ducked nor screamed.

'Inspector', he said, addressing himself to Manton who, ever correct, tried to rise to his feet without success, his chair only permitting him to assume a semi-squatting position, 'Will you kindly take charge?' Turning to the Court as a whole he went on: 'No one is to leave this Court until the police permit them to do so. No one at all. Everyone must remain in his present seat. I shall be in my room, Inspector, if you should want me.' And with that Mr. Justice Blaney got up and went out.

To say that Manton was nonplussed would be to express it mildly. Here he was in Court with a new murder on his hands and the corpse lying so close to him that he couldn't even get out of his chair. However, with an effort he did so.

'Sergeant, go up to those seats at the back and find out the name and address of that girl who screamed just before the shot was fired', he said, addressing Talper.

The latter departed to where Maisie was lying on the seat being fanned by one of the elegant young wolves, whom Jakes had earlier noticed, and by her father who was smoothing her forehead.

Manton moved to the far side of the table to have a word with Alan Sands.

'I don't think you need bother to stay, sir. I know I can always find you at your Chambers. I happened to be looking straight past you at that girl who screamed when the shot was fired, so I think I can rule you out as a suspect.'

Sir Genser was similarly permitted to go after making a little speech to the Inspector about giving every assistance within his power. Although Manton hadn't noticed the Old Fake when the shot was fired, he'd seen him emerge from his cover and he couldn't imagine that Sir Genser had been able to see very much of what had gone on from behind there.

Manton next went over to one of the door officers and asked him to phone the Yard for an officer of the photographic branch.

'Well, I might as well make a start with the jury, some of them must have seen something', he murmured to himself. When he looked at them, however, he saw only eleven rather apprehensive people. The foreman was missing—yes, that was the little man with the thick, gold-rimmed spectacles—now what had happened to him? The answer to this question was provided by Alfred Knight, the usher who sat outside in the Judges' corridor and who was the rapper on the door when the Judge was about to enter. He was a fat bald-headed old man who now puffed up to Manton.

'I know what happened to the foreman', he panted, as though reading Manton's thoughts. 'I was sitting in my usual place at the end of the corridor when I heard the shot. I started out of my seat thinking it came from the next Court down and I was on my way along there when he shot out of this door.' At this point Alfred Knight pointed at the door nearest to the jury box which led into the Judges' corridor where lay the Judges' rooms and the jury retiring rooms. This door was at the jury box end of the Judges' bench and at the other was a similar one which was by the seats where Maisie Jenks was sitting and was the one through which the Judge made his ceremonial entry on each occasion.

'Do you mean the juror left through that door?' asked Manton.

'Yes, yes', said Knight, breathless and excited. 'We met in the corridor just about behind the Judges' seat and he spoke to me.'

'What did he say?'

'He said something about shooting and then he added something like: "I saw him do it and he pointed the gun at me." He never stopped and he dashed on past me.'

'Did you see where he went?'

'No I couldn't. I came into Court through the door he'd used and I suppose he turned right by my seat and went out there.' He pointed in the direction of the doors which separate the private from the public part of the building. 'The officer on that door will be able to tell you where he went. I expect he saw him and he probably stopped him leaving.'

'I hope so', said Manton without much confidence. The confusion had been so great that it seemed more than likely that Mr. Pinty had been able to slip out without anyone paying any heed to him. Anyway Manton presumed that he would be able to find him at his home, but it was tiresome that an eye-witness had got into such a panic that he'd fled before anyone had fully realized what had happened.

Manton looked around the Court and wondered just what to tackle next. It really was a quite fantastic situation and one which no police manual dealt with. By now there was a uniformed officer at each of the doors which led from the Court, and people, having recovered from their first shock with that merciful resilience with which providence has endowed the human race, were now talking to each other in excited little whispers, while Tarrant still lay, a crumpled heap, where he'd been so suddenly slain. Much to Manton's surprise no one made any attempt to move. They were like a well-disciplined class awaiting their teacher's word that lessons for the day were over and they could now go home, but no playing on the way. One or two women were being assiduously fanned by their neighbours, but otherwise the scene was ridiculously normal except for the corpse which many were now straining to get a better view of.

Manton cleared his throat.

'I'm sorry to have to detain you all here, ladies and gentlemen, but I hope it won't be for very much longer. As soon as some further C.I.D. officers arrive, I shall ask everyone to give his name and address and then you'll be able to go home, and we can get in touch with you later if we want to. Meanwhile if anyone saw anything of what happened when the shot was fired, I'd be glad if he'd come forward straight away.'

There had been complete quiet as he spoke and all attention had been riveted on him. As he finished his little address he turned and faced the jury, MacBruce and Jakes Hartman; it was from this quarter that he expected to receive help. Someone amongst them must have seen something of importance, if not the whole thing. The silence which had fallen when he began to speak continued, however, with everyone looking expectantly at everyone else and nobody showing any inclination to take the limelight. MacBruce sat stolidly in his little box gazing abstractedly at the body which lay only a couple of feet from him. Jakes Hartman, for his part, was looking anxiously towards Maisie who was now sitting up sipping at a glass of water. Her father supported her and Sergeant Talper was apparently busy with notebook and pencil. The jury were now the chief centre of general interest and they were looking slightly conscious of the fact and of the further fact that one of their number (indeed, their foreman) had vanished suddenly from their midst.

After giving instructions to the half-dozen C.I.D. men who'd just arrived, and getting the photographer on to the job of photographing the scene from every conceivable angle, Manton decided that he'd better tackle the jury himself and try and thaw them into speech. He was pretty certain that once their tongues were loosed, he'd have difficulty in making them stop talking at all. That incredible-looking female who sat behind the missing Mr. Pinty for example, he couldn't believe that she'd be reticent when she saw the chance of being spotlighted in the drama. In fact, she'd probably be selling her story to the Sunday papers before he knew where he was. Manton stepped over the body and gingerly went up the four steps which brought him to the level of the jury and witness boxes.

'Excuse me, madam, may I have your name please?'

'Miss Fenwick-Blunt and I live at the Rivercroft Private Hotel in South Kensington.'

Just the sort of place I'd expect you to live, thought Manton. Miss Fenwick-Blunt had raised her lorgnette and appeared to be examining his bottom waistcoat button with interest.

'Well, Miss Fenwick-Blunt, perhaps you'll tell me exactly what you saw occur.'

That ought to unlock the flood gates, he thought as he spoke. But Miss Fenwick-Blunt remained silent, still apparently fascinated by the Inspector's mid-line. Then she slowly raised her eyes, cast a slow look round the Court and finally rested her gaze on Manton's patiently hopeful face. He got the impression that this rather bizarre-looking woman had been thinking out with care exactly what she was going to say. And if he expected an excited and voluble eye-witness account which would lead to an immediate arrest, he was going to be disappointed.

'I really saw nothing, Inspector,' she said with sudden decision, 'absolutely nothing.'

'Oh, come, madam, you must have seen something. After all, this man was shot only a couple of yards away from you and he was facing you at the time.'

'Oh yes, I was looking at him until there was that scream and then I looked to where it had come from and didn't see the prisoner—er, poor Mr. Tarrant—until he was lying on the ground.'

'Miss Fenwick-Blunt, I want you to think very carefully; can you give me any idea as to who fired that shot?'

37

'None. I know it wasn't me but otherwise I can't help you, Inspector.'

Manton had feared all along that he was going to find that the girl's scream had so distracted everyone, that no one had looked at Tarrant until it was all over. It was diabolical and there must be some connection between the scream and the shot which he would later have to investigate. It just couldn't have been a coincidence.

Manton turned again to Miss Fenwick-Blunt. He was already beginning to feel frustrated but knew it would be fatal to show any such emotion at this stage. His voice was still patient.

'You must have seen the juror in front of you go out; can you help about that?'

'No, all I know is that immediately after the shot I was aware of his very rapid departure through that door there on the left.' With a maddening half-smile she added: 'I'm afraid I must disappoint you, Inspector, if you think I am going to say that I saw Mr. Pinty shoot Mr. Tarrant and then run for his life, because I just didn't. He seemed such a quiet little man, I'm sure he'd never murder anyone.'

Manton decided there was no point in questioning this tiresome woman further. He was quite sure she was not being frank, though her explanation for not having seen anything was perfectly reasonable in the circumstances. It was rather the way she spoke that caused him to make a mental note that he would want to see her again fairly soon, and he reflected grimly that he'd penetrate that armour of calm confidence of hers if he had to use thumbscrews to do it.

Manton saw that the officer who had been taking

photographs was trying to attract his attention. He descended to the last step—the step which Tarrant never ascended and where his body now lay stretched between it and Manton's chair at the centre table.

'See that, sir', said the photographer pointing beneath Manton's chair. The latter's gaze followed the pointing finger. There on the floor lay the neat cold shape of a German Luger pistol.

This was almost too much for Manton. Not only had someone apparently been murdered a couple of feet behind his back but the weapon now lay under the chair on which he'd been sitting at the time.

It might save trouble if I confessed at once and arrested myself, he ruefully thought. It occurred to him, however, that he wasn't going to do any good with the Court full of goggling people who had been watching hawk-like every movement he'd been making. It was a novel experience for them to be present at a murder and watch the police initiate their investigation. They'd be the envy of their streets for weeks to come. Some would doubtless give themselves important parts in the drama which they would describe *ad nauseam* to their friends and relations, while these in turn would bask in as much of the reflected glory as they could conveniently appropriate to themselves. 'Yes, I gave the Inspector a hand —but he asked me to keep it to myself for the present', and so on. Others would go to the other extreme and play it all down till it sounded like a rather tedious everyday affair with the police doing their usual laborious bit of bungling.

Manton went and had a word with Talper and then standing in the well of the Court announced: 'All right, everyone may now leave and we'll doubtless be getting into touch with many of you within the next few days. If you should be leaving the addresses which you've given to the police, would you please let me know at Scotland Yard where you can be found.' He turned to Jakes Hartman and MacBruce. 'I'd like to speak to you two before you go.'

Sergeant Talper came down to the well of the Court from the seats beneath the public gallery where Manton had sent him to interview the girl who had screamed. When he had pushed his way through to where she was sitting, he had found her being revived by her father who was nursing her head in his lap, and by others around who were keenly offering suggestions on the best way to deal with young girls who had fainted. The young man on her left was telling his neighbour for the third time how he'd been casting covert glances at her and was actually deciding the exact colour of her eyes when she let out her scream and flopped forwards. He had been first to render first-aid and had not been over-pleased when her father had pushed his way through the little crowd which surrounded her and taken over the care of his daughter. On the other hand it did leave him free to join in the gaping excitement at what was taking place on the other side of the Court.

When Talper had spoken, Mr. Jenks had immediately looked up and replied: 'She's my daughter, officer. She seems to be right out. I can't think what happened to her; I don't think she's injured.'

It was obvious that he was extremely agitated, and Sergeant Talper had decided that nothing would be gained by close questioning him then and there. He just made a note of his name and address and learnt that his daughter lived there too. He had been about to return to Manton who was then talking to one of the jurors when the girl suddenly opened her eyes wide and then quickly closed them again.

'What did you find out about that girl?' asked Manton, when he rejoined him.

'Her name is Maisie Jenks and that's her father with her. They live up St. John's Wood way, and she knows who the murderer is.'

Chapter Six

'WHAT?' said Manton, startled into bad grammar.

'She knows who did it all right. She must know; because her scream must be connected with the murder.'

'Oh, I see what you mean.'

Manton's only complaint about Talper was this tendency to making somewhat dramatic statements which turned out to be without substance. One day he would speak severely to him about it.

'Her father, one Harry Jenks, was with her and said they'd be at home if required. I told him you'd probably want to see his daughter later in the day.'

'Did he give any reason for his daughter chilling our blood and then flopping out like that?'

'No, none, and I got the impression he was pretty worried about it and himself wondered what happened to make her do it.'

'So he ought to wonder', said Manton dryly. 'Well, Andy, will you take the shorthand writer, over to the other side of the Court and see what he knows? I'm going to have a word with MacBruce.'

Except for the photographer and finger-print people who were packing up, and Manton, Talper, MacBruce and Jakes Hartman, the Court was now empty.

Manton decided that a pleasant joviality as between colleagues was his best line of approach with the uniformed Inspector.

'Well, thank heavens we've got them all out of the way. Now you and I can have a chat.'

It seemed however that he was doomed to be disappointed in his witnesses that day. None of them showed that forthcomingness he hoped for and MacBruce, though a fellow policeman, was no exception. He remained quite silent as if he regarded it Manton's job to say exactly what he wanted to know before he said anything himself. Manton was nettled by his attitude.

'Well, Inspector, perhaps you'd be so good as to tell me all you know about this occurrence', he said, employing police jargon and in a tone of semi-sarcasm.

Without a smile or hint of amusement, MacBruce cleared his throat and began as if talking to a complete stranger.

'I was watching Tarrant pass in front of me when that girl screamed and I immediately looked up to where she was sitting, and saw her fall to the floor. The shot can only have been fired from someone in the jury box, and I imagine none of us is in any doubt as to who it was either.'

'Do you mean the foreman who rushed out immediately afterwards?'

'Of course; who else? Find him and you've found your murderer. I should hardly have thought you'd want to interview all these other people.'

His tone was rude and off-hand, and it was his obvious intention to convey to Manton that he thought he was wasting his time in useless inquiries. Manton saw no reason to enlighten him and tell him that an officer was already watching outside Mr. Pinty's home with instructions to phone him, Manton, at the Old Bailey as soon as he arrived there; nor to tell him what Mr.

Pinty had said to Alfred Knight, the Judge's usher, on his precipitate way out.

'Which way was Tarrant facing when he was shot?' he asked, starting out on a new tack.

MacBruce looked down at the floor where shortly before the body had lain, but where now there was only a large smeared blood stain on the brown linoleum.

'He was facing to the front, of course; towards the witness box.'

'I don't know why you should say "of course". Everyone seems to have turned towards the scream and I don't see why Tarrant should have been an exception. How do you know he didn't look round as well?'

'He couldn't have from the position his body was in. After the shot he reeled back a pace towards the back of your chair; then he fell forward with his face almost on the bottom step. If I'd put out a hand, I could have touched him as he collapsed. He was shot through the heart and it can only have come from the front.'

'Maybe you're right.'

'Find the foreman and you'll probably discover that he's a homicidal maniac who has recently escaped from Broadmoor and who thought it would be amusing to murder someone in the Court where he himself was once tried for murder.'

Manton gave the uniformed Inspector a searching look but the latter showed no inclination to share his joke, if such it was intended to be. It was clear he had made up his mind about who had done it and he wasn't disposed to humour the C.I.D. in what he considered their interminable questions and efforts to complicate the simple.

Sergeant Talper rejoined Manton.

'That shorthand writer fellow says that Tarrant was looking at MacBruce just before he was shot. He didn't see who fired the pistol.'

'No one saw who fired the pistol, Andy', said Manton bitterly. 'It's too utterly fantastic. A man is murdered just behind our innocent backs. It happens in a Court full of people, some of whom must have seen what took place, while others were in a position to pat him on the shoulder, they were so close to him; but not one person saw who fired the shot. At least, one person— and one only—saw, and he's decided not to stay and tell us.'

'Have you spoken to the warder yet?' asked Talper.

'What warder?'

'The one who was escorting Tarrant to the witness box and who was just behind him when he was shot.'

'Good heavens, yes, where the hell has he got to? Perhaps the bullet went right through Tarrant and into him, and he's gone off to have it extracted. Now you mention him, Andy, I haven't seen him at all. By what right has he taken himself off? Go and see where he's got to.'

Sergeant Talper entered the dock and disappeared down the steps which lead to the cells.

Manton was quite alone in Court. At each door a policeman was on guard and in the corridor outside the main door was a milling crowd, with a bunch of press-men in the front standing on tiptoe and looking through the double glass doors to see what was going on inside. Unfortunately for them, they couldn't see Manton who had gone to the City Lands seats beneath the public gallery and was now sitting where Maisie Jenks had been when the murder was committed. He hoped that inspiration would come to him as he looked down on the scene of the crime and the now empty Court, oblivious of the noise made by the jostling and excited crowd without. For five minutes Manton sat thus in contemplation and if Inspector MacBruce could have seen him, that officer's already pungent views on the C.I.D. would have erupted in an outburst of snorting impatience. But for Manton it was time well spent; it was the first opportunity he had had of giving the affair a little cool, dispassionate thought. When he eventually got up, he reckoned that there were no more than five people who could possibly have committed the crime, and at any rate he knew who they all were. Of course, if he could only find out why Tarrant was murdered, he would have the solution to the complete problem. But first things first, he mused, and clearly a visit to Mr. Pinty's home, and, he hoped, Mr. Pinty himself was at the top of the list.

Sergeant Talper emerged from the cells and came up into the dock. He saw Manton over where Maisie Jenks had been sitting, and went across to him.

'I've seen the warder chap—name of Glindy. His head was also apparently turned away when the shot was fired and he didn't see who did it. He says Tarrant staggered back into him before falling face forward to the floor.'

'Why did he disappear like that afterwards?'

'He says quite frankly that he was so shaken and felt so physically sick that he just re-entered the dock and went down to the cells.'

'Even if that's true,' said Manton, 'his reason I mean, it's highly irregular. There he is, closest to Tarrant, and by way of being his official guard and escort, and as soon

46

as his charge needs some help, he buzzes off to go and be sick in a basin. Was he in fact sick?'

'I don't know. I didn't ask him that point blank, and, er—I didn't look for any evidence of the fact.'

'Well, Andy, I reckon there's just one more person we must have a word with before we leave this building and that's the officer on that door outside.' Manton indicated with a nod of his head the swing doors which separated the public corridor outside the Court from the carpeted passage which led to the rooms used by the Judges and City dignitaries. 'Pinty must have passed him on his way out and we'll find out if he said anything. See if you can find him will you, he's probably still on duty at one of these doors.'

Sergeant Talper, the ever *fidus* Achates, departed once more and Manton started collecting up his papers from the table in the well of the Court. The Tarrant case had reached a premature end in one sense, but it was only just starting in another. Tarrant had been a colourful character in the world of crime, and he and the police had always maintained friendly relations. He had seldom borne them any ill-will when they felt compelled to step in and restrict his activities. That did not mean that he always obliged them by confessing to whatever the particular offence of the moment might be. Far from it. The police knew that they had to prove their case against him up to the hilt by outside evidence, without any Trojan horse assistance prompted by his conscience. Once an over zealous officer had decided that force was the only way to deal with Tarrant and his likes, but his action only brought Tarrant an acquittal and himself a stern rebuke and almost expulsion from the Force. And now Tarrant had departed this life with suddenness and in a manner quite unfitting his character. Someone had once described him as a sort of Raffles without that august gentleman's altruism and perennial good fortune.

Sergeant Talper came back into Court through the door which was used by the more senior Counsel and those using the City Lands seats. He was followed by a grey-haired and rather portly police constable of the City Police Force who looked distinctly uncomfortable. Manton gave him a friendly smile.

'This is P.C. Yates who was on duty at the door in question', said Talper.

'Oh fine', said Manton. 'Did you see this juror leave, Yates? I imagine he must have gone by you to get out.'

Manton in fact had wondered why the constable hadn't stopped Pinty from leaving, but refrained from putting this into words as Yates looked so unhappy. The latter cleared his throat and spoke.

'I'm afraid, sir, I didn't see him leave.' Manton raised his eyebrows and the other went on: 'You see, sir, as soon as the shot rang out the Under-Sheriff, who was in his room down the corridor, ran out into the passage and called to me. And so, sir, I left my seat by the double doors and went along to him.' He paused. 'I can only suppose that this juror went out into the public corridor when I was going to the Under-Sheriff's room and of course I wouldn't then have seen him.' There was another pause and he said: 'I'm terribly sorry about this, sir; I feel all sorts of a fool and I suppose I must expect to get a good sharp rap over the knuckles.'

Manton felt every sympathy for the constable who was undoubtedly very down in the mouth at the way things had turned out.

'Oh, don't worry. I don't really see that there was anything particularly reprehensible in leaving your post in the circumstances. After all, you can't very well ignore an Under-Sheriff.'

Yates brightened at Manton's friendly words.

'Of course, sir, if I had been at my place, I wouldn't have let him go past; I'd have stopped him. As it is, I've probably let the murderer get away.'

He fell into a gloomy silence again.

'Oh, and why do you say the murderer?' asked Manton quickly.

'Well that seems to be the general talk, sir, that this juror—Pinty was his name, wasn't it?—shot Tarrant and then escaped in the confusion.'

Manton turned to Sergeant Talper.

'I think it's time for us to leave the scene of the crime and take ourselves out to Edgware to see this Mr. Pinty. Let's be off.'

Chapter Seven

MRS. PINTY was washing up the lunch things when Manton and Talper arrived at the house. Since Malcolm had his mid-day meal at school and her husband was always out, she seldom sat down to more than a frugal piece of bread and cheese. She never bothered to cook herself anything beyond a cup of tea and she always looked forward to the half hour afterwards, when she could sit down and look at the paper before resuming the never-ending domestic chores from which a conscientious suburban housewife seldom finds relief.

Wonder who that can be, she thought, as the bell rang. She dried the plate she had just been washing, wiped her hands and went into the hall to the front door. On the doorstep she saw two men. Superior salesmen, she immediately conjectured.

'Good afternoon', she said, politely and questioningly.

'Are you Mrs. Pinty, madam?' asked the younger of the two. Mrs. Pinty thought he had a pleasant friendly face and was rejecting the salesman theory when he went on: 'I'm Detective Chief Inspector Manton from Scotland Yard and this is Detective Sergeant Talper. Is your husband at home, Mrs. Pinty?'

Mrs. Pinty's heart missed a beat as visions of some ghastly accident sprang to her mind's eye. Perhaps Malcolm had been knocked down and hurt; or Cynthia had collapsed at the hospital. Come to think of it, she had looked a bit pale recently. She tried, however, to keep the note of anxiety out of her voice when she replied.

'No, I'm afraid he's not. He never gets back till about half-past six. And as a matter of fact to-day he's on a jury at the Old Bailey.'

The quick glance which the two officers exchanged did not escape her and she fervently wished they'd tell her what they wanted.

More thoughts flashed through her mind but none of them gave her any reassurance.

'You must tell me, Inspector, what's happened and why you want my husband.'

Manton appeared to cogitate this question for a brief moment and then, as if suddenly making up his mind, he looked straight into her face and spoke.

'I think, madam, it would be better if we could come inside.' After they were seated in the front room and Mrs. Pinty had turned on one bar of the electric fire, he went on: 'A man was murdered in Court at the Old Bailey this morning, and almost immediately afterwards your husband left the Court in rather strange circumstances.' He observed the scared look that passed across her face and quickly added:

'I'm not suggesting for a moment that your husband had anything to do with it—I mean, that it was he who did the shooting—but he's obviously a very material witness and I want to get in touch with him absolutely as soon as possible.'

Mrs. Pinty said nothing for a few moments and Manton was grateful to her for not giving way to hysterics or breaking down. Years of similar interviews had not hardened him to such scenes and he always found them extremely distasteful. When Mrs. Pinty did speak her voice was tremulous but under control, though obviously only with a considerable effort, for which Manton admired her all the more. He reckoned she was about forty-five. Her hair was an undistinguished grey and had been waved not long ago. She had naturally rosy cheeks and wore no make-up. Her hands were rough and coarse from being constantly in and out of washing-up water.

'I hardly know what to say, Inspector. My husband left here shortly before nine o'clock this morning to go to the Court and I was not expecting him back till this evening.'

'Well perhaps we could wait a short while to see if he comes back and meanwhile you could give us a few particulars.'

Sergeant Talper, who had been making notes of the interchange between Manton and Mrs. Pinty, turned over a page of his notebook and, with pencil poised, waited expectantly.

'Did your husband tell you anything about the case he was trying, Mrs. Pinty?'

'No, he was very quiet about it when he got in last night.' Then thinking that this remark might possibly be misinterpreted, Mrs. Pinty added hastily: 'I mean he was always very quiet and he didn't tell me much about the case because he said the Judge had told them not to discuss it.' With a reflective little smile, she recalled how she'd been somewhat irked by his discretion and refusal to tell her about it. 'In fact, Inspector, I tried to get some of the details out of him and was a bit niggled when he told me to read about it in the evening papers.'

She seems to be telling the truth, thought Manton

and said: 'And this morning when he left, did he appear quite normal?'

'Yes, perfectly.'

'Nothing on his mind or anything like that?'

'Oh no, nothing at all.'

'I'm sorry to have to pry like this, but I'm sure you understand that I have my duty to do.'

Mrs. Pinty nodded her appreciation of the situation.

'Did your husband have any enemies, or were there times when he was away from home for certain periods?'

'I'm sure John had no enemies and his work never took him away from London.' As if in answer to Manton's further question, she continued: 'And he always came home every evening. Once a week we usually went to the pictures but otherwise we generally stopped in.'

It seemed to Manton that the Pintys were (at least outwardly) a typical suburban family living a very ordinary routine existence. Long experience in the police had however taught him the truth of the adage that still waters run deep. He knew how, even in a peaceful suburban setting, a sudden eruption could sometimes reveal the basest human passions and drama of unremitted sordidness. He looked about the room. It was cold and unlived-in and obviously used only when entertaining company on rare occasions. A paper frill affair hid the grate and discreet lace curtains shut out the inquisitive eyes of the neighbours. On the walls were two hideous monstrosities. One was presumably a Victorian member of the family, when young, dressed in a sailor suit: on his face was the simpering expression of a doted-on child. The other was a portrait of another

53

Victorian relation, this time a fragile female in the early twenties who was casting a yearning gaze out of a window. Over the mantelpiece, rather surprisingly, was a photographic reproduction of Tintoretto's *Susannah and the Elders*. Manton wondered how it came to be there and what Mr. and Mrs. Pinty thought of it. Did they have it because it was a picture that pleased their senses or did they take it for granted like the waste-paper basket?

By now it seemed to Manton almost a certainty that John Pinty was a murderer and he was fortified by the knowledge that before coming out to Edgware he had circulated a description of the missing man which had been specially notified to sea and air ports. In these circumstances it was hardly likely that Mr. Pinty would arrive home and he had never really expected to find him there. Mrs. Pinty had impressed him by her simple straightforwardness and he now felt more sorry for her than ever. There was always the chance that Mr. Pinty would try and make contact with his wife, and again Manton had laid his plans accordingly. He got up preparatory to leaving and suddenly felt unutterably tired. He had a violent headache; a murder had been committed within a couple of feet of him in a packed Court but no one had seen it happen. Well he couldn't just sit back and wait for Mr. Pinty to be found. He mightn't ever be found and meanwhile there were other lines which had to be followed up. But why had he wanted to kill Tarrant so urgently that he was prepared to do it before a large and concentrated audience and run the almost certain risk of immediate arrest? It was indeed ironical that he had defied fate and for the moment got away with it. The telephone ringing broke in on these thoughts. Mrs. Pinty got up from her chair without a word and left the room. She re-entered a moment or two later.

'It's for you, Inspector. In the hall.'

This'll be news of Pinty, thought Manton ever hopeful as he went out. But it was only a message that the Assistant Commissioner wished to see him at the Yard as soon as possible.

Chapter Eight

INSPECTOR MACBRUCE walked into his home just about the time that Inspector Manton and Sergeant Talper were leaving Edgware. His wife, a rather sullen woman with an unexpressive hard face and hair pulled into a tight bun at the back, was coming downstairs to go out and do some shopping.

'Why are you back at this hour?'

It was a bleak question asked without any hint of pleasure at her husband's unexpected return. Like him, she also came from Scotland and detested London where she'd had to live these last twenty years, and more particularly the drab south-London area with its clanking, heaving trams, where they had their home. She had married her husband to get away from a life of drudgery on the lonely Highland farm where she'd been born. For most of the time she and Robert MacBruce tolerated each other in dour silence.

'There's been a murder at the Court and everything's closed down.' Mrs. MacBruce seemed quite uninterested in this startling piece of news and made as if to continue her journey to the front door. 'I'm not sure that fool Manton doesn't suspect me of committing it.'

Mrs. MacBruce halted and stared stonily at her husband who'd just made this challenging remark.

'Tarrant?' she said cryptically.

'Yes, shot dead within a few feet of me just as he was about to go into the witness box.' Mrs. MacBruce now appeared more interested in the affair and, without a

56

word, turned away from the front door and went along
to the kitchen. Her husband followed her. 'The foreman
of the jury disappeared suddenly, immediately afterwards and they're still searching for him. Of course it
was him who did it, but,' and here the Inspector paused
a moment, 'but don't be surprised if that smoothy,
Inspector Manton, comes buzzing round here full of
questions. I thought you'd better just know how the
land lies.'

Without so much as a word, Mrs. MacBruce left the
kitchen and, a second after, her husband heard the front
door slam. Alone in the house, he went upstairs to their
bedroom. He opened the bottom drawer in the dressing-
table and feeling beneath a pile of woollen underwear,
pulled out a Smith and Wesson .38 revolver. From the
opposite end of the drawer he extracted a small carton
of ammunition. Putting both in his pocket he went
downstairs again and left the house.

After the police had left the Old Bailey, Jakes hung
around for some time not knowing what to do with himself. He had made a full statement, but after waiting an
hour or so, he decided he couldn't stand the atmosphere
any longer and certainly he wasn't able to concentrate
his mind on anything but Maisie Jenks and the where-
fore of her scream.

It was somehow like being the sole survivor in a town
that had suddenly been struck by an elemental hurri-
cane which left not only physical destruction in its
wake, but swept away man's mental sheet anchors and
left him in a wilderness of hopeless unreality. So it was
that Jakes decided to creep home to try to compose his
thoughts and make up his mind about the immediate

future. He told a colleague where the police could find him if they wanted him and left the building which had now assumed such a sinister character. Somehow he managed to get on the right bus, but he hardly noticed the journey back to Bayswater and all the way his thoughts danced uncontrollably about his head.

After alighting, he decided that as a first measure to regaining a normal outlook, he must ring up Maisie, and with this end in view he entered the public call box, from which he always phoned her. He dialled and the bell at the other end seemed to ring interminably. At last the receiver was lifted.

'Yes, who's that?'

The voice sounded displeased at having to answer the phone and there was nothing inviting or friendly in its tone.

'It's Jakes Hartman speaking. May I please speak to Miss Maisie Jenks?'

'Oh good afternoon, Mr. Hartman. I don't think we've met. I'm Maisie's father.' Jakes had already guessed this, but before he had time to make an inane and non-committal reply to this information, Mr. Jenks went on: 'I'm afraid you can't speak to Maisie now. She's better but still not well enough to talk to anyone on the telephone.'

Jakes quickly deliberated whether to pound him with the armoury of questions that besieged his mind. But he didn't know Mr. Jenks, and though he had sounded slightly more civil when he learnt who it was making the call, he was obviously in no mood to submit to a searching cross-examination about his daughter's behaviour.

'I'll ring back later, Mr. Jenks', said Jakes not without a note of regret and dropped the receiver.

He left the call box and slowly traced his footsteps to the boarding house where he had a room. He let himself in with his own key, and, praying that he wouldn't be intercepted by any of the inquisitive old ladies who were his fellow-lodgers, shot up the stairs and with a sigh of relief gained his room and shut the door.

He lit the gas fire and, loosening his tie and collar, slumped down into the only armchair to think. For a time the sole question which went round and round his head was why had Maisie screamed and fainted just before Tarrant was shot, and who was it that had killed Tarrant. The latter had been almost within touching distance of Jakes when he was so suddenly and violently murdered. It could only have been the foreman of the jury who did it. Because if it wasn't him, why did he vanish in the way he did? That wasn't the behaviour of an innocent man. But then again it could have been MacBruce, he was close enough to do it and Tarrant was facing MacBruce when he was killed, just as Jakes had told the police he was. Glindy could have done it too, but why should any of them have wanted to do it? And what had made Maisie scream? So the one thought revolved about his head without his seeming to get any further forward in his mental reconstruction of the crime.

Not very far away at Scotland Yard others were also going over the crime in detail. They also had compiled a list of possible murderers, but theirs contained a further name, that of Jakes Hartman.

Miss Fenwick-Blunt had a healthy appetite and it was unlike her to miss a meal. Thus, the genteel manageress of the hotel where she lived was surprised when she said she was going out and wouldn't be back to dinner. The manageress had no idea that Miss Fenwick-Blunt had been a member of the jury in the Tarrant case, it being one of the few details which wasn't plastered over the front page of the evening papers. She regarded Miss Fenwick-Blunt as typical of the garrulous spinsters who infested the hotel and she would indeed have been surprised if she had known just how many secrets Miss Fenwick-Blunt kept to herself and just how untypical she was.

Outside in the street, Miss Fenwick-Blunt hailed a taxi and directed the driver to take her to a certain Church in South London where she wished to be dropped. To say that the driver was surprised would be to put it mildly, but without comment he turned the clock to one and threepence and started off on the strange assignment. It took about thirty-five minutes to get there and Miss Fenwick-Blunt paid him off and waited at the kerbside till he drove away. Then she studied an address on the back of an old envelope which she took from her bag and crossed the road and dived at a surprisingly brisk pace down a side street of small semi-detached houses, glancing quickly at the numbers as she went. About half-way down, she stopped outside a house which was no different from its neighbours and looked it up and down. The road was empty and ill-lit, though brightly lighted buses could be seen passing the end from where she had walked, and the noise of the traffic along the main road drifted down to where she now stood. A cat ran across and jumped up on to the wall: it was closely followed by another and larger cat. Miss Fenwick-Blunt stepped up to the front door of number forty-six and gave one short sharp knock. After a few moments the door was cautiously opened and she disappeared inside. Once more the street was deserted. About twenty minutes later the front door of Number forty-six opened again and Miss Fenwick-Blunt came out and, without so much as a backward glance, turned out of the little front gate and with purposeful steps returned the way she'd come. As she left the house, a curtain in the front room was discreetly pulled aside and the pale nervous face of Prison Officer Albert Glindy watched her departure.

The Assistant Commissioner (Crime) had called a conference at the Yard for eight-thirty that evening and it was just a minute or two before Big Ben struck the hour that Manton knocked on his door and entered. It was a nice spacious office overlooking the Thames and one in which the perdition of a good many criminals had been successfully planned.

'Any news of Pinty, yet?' asked the Assistant Commissioner as Manton moved across the room.

'None, sir. He's just vanished into thin air. I was on to the local station just before I came along and they report all quiet on his home front. Mrs. Pinty hasn't left the house since I was there this afternoon. The boy's come back from school and the daughter's arrived there too now. She's training to be a nurse at the Prince Charles Hospital, and her mother was going to ring her up when I left this afternoon.'

'Of course Pinty may have telephoned his wife without our knowing.'

Manton smiled.

'No, sir. I've checked on that as well and had all calls to the house tapped. We've got a chap at the exchange and two on duty in the street where the house is. I don't think it's possible for Pinty to get in touch with his wife by any means without our knowing about it.'

'No, I agree. It seems, Manton, as if you've covered that particular aspect with your usual thoroughness.'

The Assistant Commissioner was a rather austere looking man and a good many of his subordinates had a wholesome respect for him bordering on fear. He was immensely hard-working and efficient as well, but he'd long held a high opinion of Manton, and in fact it was he who had been the cause of his rapid promotion in the force. Manton was not one of those who was afraid of him.

'Has Dr. Craig done the post mortem yet?'

'Yes, sir, he finished about an hour ago. Tarrant was shot clean through the heart, the bullet's path being in a slightly right to left direction; i.e. sir, at the time he was murdered, Tarrant wasn't facing square to the killer but was turned slightly to the left.'

'What range does Craig give the shot?'

'Close—which of course we know. But there were no powder burns on his clothing at all. It couldn't have been less than two feet and not more than about ten feet.'

'From all that, I gather the wound is quite consistent with a shot fired from where Pinty was sitting.'

'Yes, sir, that's so,' replied Manton slowly, and after a pause, 'but it doesn't rule out others having fired the fatal shot.' The Assistant Commissioner gave him a long, studied look. He knew him well enough to know that he didn't just advance such thoughts or theories without a reason. Manton went on slowly, apparently

picking his words with care: 'I realize, sir, that this
may sound surprising to you, and I agree that at first
sight, if not at second sight as well, Pinty is obviously
our man. But until we find Pinty, I think it would be
wrong to concentrate solely on that theory. If he did do
it, at the moment we have no idea why he did it. In fact
from what we've been able to learn about him, he would
seem to be the last person to commit a murder.' The
Assistant Commissioner was about to interject a remark
but Manton went on quickly: 'Oh, I know, sir, that the
Pintys of this world do commit murders from time to
time. But usually they strangle their nagging wives after
having put up with them for numberless years—not
shoot someone dead in as dramatic circumstances as
any detective story writer could conjure up. As I say,
there's no earthly or apparent reason why Pinty wanted
to murder Tarrant, and further, the method and execution were quite out of keeping with his character as we
know it.'

A deep silence followed this short exposition of Manton's ideas on the crime. Sergeant Talper sat silent as
he always did on such occasions. He was very content
to play second fiddle to the Inspector at these con-
ferences.

The Assistant Commissioner cleared his throat. 'Yes,
but everything points to Pinty, and I, for one, believe
that when we find him, we shall have gone a very long
way to solving this matter. After all if he had nothing to
do with it, why did he rush away like that?'

'He told the Judge's usher that someone had pointed
the pistol at him after the murder.'

The Assistant Commissioner made a derisive noise.
'Well, even if that's true, why didn't he go straight

63

along to a Police Station when he got outside the Old Bailey? There's only one logical answer to that, you know, Manton. The answer that British juries know to give when they're trying murder cases.'

'I can see, sir, that you don't think much of my other theories. At least they're scarcely theories. But I still think that at this stage I would be wrong in excluding other possibilities. You see, sir, it would be so much easier if we had some evidence as to which direction Tarrant was facing at the precise moment he was shot. But not a soul in Court was apparently looking at him and for all we know, he, like others, had turned round when that girl screamed. If he did, then it couldn't have been Pinty who shot him.'

The Assistant Commissioner sighed.

'Well, Manton, you're in charge of this case and you know you have my complete confidence. It's up to you to conduct the investigation on the lines you think best. While I wouldn't myself bother with other theories if I were in charge, I'm far from saying that I think you're wrong to do so.'

'It's very nice of you to put it that way, sir.'

'Now what about this girl who screamed? Why did she scream? Surely she saw something.'

·'Sergeant Talper has seen her and I'm going out to the Jenks' house immediately after this conference. Up to the present she has told us nothing useful. She was pretty upset when Talper saw her in Court immediately after the murder, and said she couldn't remember anything. But I'm hoping her memory will have improved by the time I see her.'

The telephone on the Assistant Commissioner's desk rang and he lifted the receiver.

'For you', he said, handing the instrument to Manton.

'Hello, Detective Chief Inspector Manton here. Oh, good evening, Mr. Jenks. I was just about to come out and see you.'

The other occupants of the room could only hear the odd metallic noises coming down the line which always sound such birdlike gibberish unless you have the receiver to your ear. They watched Manton's face and saw his expression turn to a puzzled frown.

'I'll come over straight away, Mr. Jenks', he said and placed the receiver back on the instrument and turned to face the expectant company. 'Maisie Jenks has disappeared.' No one spoke and he went on: 'Her father left her in her room about tea-time. She was in bed and wanted to go to sleep. A few minutes ago Mr. Jenks went up to see how she was. He tip-toed into her room, not wanting to wake her if she was still asleep, but he found her bed empty and the room in comparative disorder. It looked as if she had hurriedly flung a few things into a case and taken a powder like Mr. Pinty.'

'Any note left?' asked the Assistant Commissioner.

'Apparently not. And no one saw her leave. Her father was in his study at the back of the house and didn't hear anyone go out. Young Jenks, the brother, was out and the only servant was down in the basement kitchen; and anyway she's stone deaf.'

'Mrs. Jenks?' asked the Assistant Commissioner laconically.

'There's isn't one. He's a widower, I understand. Anyway there's no Mrs. Jenks living at the house.'

'I expect you want to get up there right away, so we'll adjourn our conference.'

Manton and Sergeant Talper ran through the august building and out to their car. As they turned out on to the Embankment, Manton said : 'If it goes on like this, there soon won't be anyone left for us to interview.'

Chapter Nine

MANTON and Talper spent a couple of hours at the Jenks' house in St. John's Wood, and when they left, Manton felt he was not much further forward. Harry Jenks was obviously worried about his daughter's sudden disappearance and he urged the two officers to find her as quickly as possible. In fact he went so far as to suggest that the search for her ought to have first priority on Manton's time, and that it was more important and urgent to find Maisie and restore her to her father than to try and find the murderer of Tarrant. Manton dismissed his anxiety as natural in the circumstances.

It was the first opportunity he had had of speaking to Jenks about the events in Number One Court that morning, and he learnt how Jenks and his daughter had often talked about attending a trial at the Old Bailey but had done nothing about it until Maisie had become friendly with young Hartman, who had offered to get them into a murder trial. It all sounded very normal and innocent, though somehow it left Manton with an odd impression which troubled his sixth sense. When he had asked Jenks about his daughter's scream in Court, the latter had replied that he was as worried as the Inspector was about it. He agreed that it must have had something to do with the shooting, though thank goodness, he had added with a forced laugh, it was quite clear that she at any rate had not committed the murder. He suggested to the Inspector that she might have seen who fired the shot, but immediately he went on to dash this theory to the ground. It was inconceivable that she alone in Court should have seen the murderer about to act when no one else had apparently seen what had happened and Manton realized that Harry Jenks was undoubtedly curious to know just what the police had found out in connection with the affair. It had so happened that when his daughter let out her dramatic scream (a scream which was the cause of all Manton's trouble) he, Jenks, had been studying the Judge's robes. He had finished the interview by telling the Inspector what a bad business it was and that he would be only too glad to help in any way that lay within his power.

As they drove away Manton turned to Sergeant Talper. 'Well, what do you think of our Mr. Jenks, Andy?'

'Not an easy person to sum up. For a time I felt he was quite genuine; but by the end I wasn't so sure. I can't tell you exactly what it was but I felt he was deliberately trying to create a certain impression for our benefit.'

'Funny you should say that. At least, I suppose not funny at all but quite natural seeing we've both been trained in the same school, but I felt the same thing.'

'He seemed genuinely worried about his daughter but his attitude about what happened in Court seemed a bit unreal to me.'

'Yes, and he seemed quite unshocked or unsurprised about it. One might almost think that he saw people shot dead in our Courts several times a week.' Manton gazed out of the window and went on: 'I must say this one deserves to go down in the annals, whatever its outcome. A man is murdered just behind our backs and in full view of one of Her Majesty's Judges and various learned Counsel, not to mention a host of more ordinary citizens. An arrest might have been expected within a matter of seconds, and yet after several hours we're only further away than we were at the beginning. Well perhaps there'll be some news of Pinty when we get back to the Yard.'

But there wasn't. Only a message to say that a lady was waiting to see Manton in his office. Now who the devil can that be? he thought, as he went along the corridor. He turned the handle of his door and entered, with the faithful Talper just behind him. Sitting in one of the chairs and looking perfectly at home was Miss Fenwick-Blunt.

'Ah, good evening, Inspector, I was told you wouldn't be long so I said I'd wait. Like Daniel, you see, I've come straight into the lion's den. But perhaps we ordinary law-abiding folk oughtn't to regard Scotland Yard as a lion's den at all—at any rate not those of us with clear consciences.'

She laughed at her own remark and, despite her use of the simile, quite clearly didn't regard herself a female Daniel, let alone Manton a lion. She still wore the hunter's green dress she'd worn in Court earlier in the day, and on her head was the same green hat covered with highly coloured feathers that made her so resemble some exotic bird out of a Brazilian jungle. When the officers had entered the room, she had remained seated but had raised her single-lens lorgnette to survey them through her right eye as she spoke. Her face was of a vague purple colour and the small veins at the sides of her ample nose showed through little clots of powder which had been liberally applied to that part of her face.

Manton was tired and in no mood for coy badinage with middle-aged spinsters. He couldn't imagine what had brought her to see him at this hour (it was nearly eleven o'clock), but he was quite certain that it wasn't anything which would be likely to help him solve the case.

'Well, Miss Blunt, it's late, and I expect you want to get back home so perhaps you'll tell me what's brought you here.'

In fact Miss Fenwick-Blunt couldn't have looked less like wanting to go home, but she smiled at the Inspector's tone.

'Its' something about that dreadful murder', she said in a confidential tone, as if expecting Manton to seize up with surprise at the information. Silly old fool, he thought, what else would bring her here. I don't suppose she's got anything to say at all; she's probably just dropped in to have a cosy chat about crime. Aloud he said : 'What is it about the murder you've come to tell us—it's not about Mr. Pinty, I suppose?'

'No, it's not about Mr. Pinty, it's about somebody else who was in Court at the time.'

Great heavens, thought Manton, will she never come to the point. It seemed in fact as if Miss Fenwick-Blunt was enjoying her visit to the utmost and was in no hurry to say her piece and depart. She continued to hold her lorgnettes to her eye as she spoke, and was obviously either blissfully unaware of Manton's searing thoughts or else calmly indifferent to them.

'Yes, Inspector, since I got back to my hotel this afternoon, I've been thinking hard about the terrible affair. Surely, I said to myself, there must have been something you noticed but forgot to mention to the Inspector. Some little detail perhaps which seems so trivial to you but which may help that young detective to solve the whole case and cover himself with glory.' She paused and beamed at Manton like a benevolent aunt. 'And now I've come to tell you that I have remembered a small matter which was clean out of my mind when we had our talk before. Of course it may be of no consequence, but I said to myself it's your duty, Victoria, to go straight along to Scotland Yard and report it in person. No good trying to do these things over the telephone.'

Manton was fast becoming numbed by her circumlocution and decided he would just sit and wait and hope for as long as he could without bursting with exasperation. In the end she might even drive him to sleep.

She seemed to be surprised by his silence but this was no more than a momentary deterrent.

'Well, Inspector,' she went on naïvely, 'I expect you'll be wondering what it is that I've come to tell you about. It's to do with the pistol.' Manton managed to look interested at this, and Sergeant Talper opened his notebook again and licked his pencil. 'Mind you, I can't absolutely swear to what I'm going to say but the more I've thought about it, the more I'm sure I'm right in coming to see you.'

We're off again, thought Manton, but brought himself to say with some energy: 'What about the pistol, Miss Blunt? It may be very important. That'll be for us to judge but please tell me at once what it is.'

'Well now, mind you, Inspector, I can't say I

71

definitely saw it, but somehow I think I did. You know how confusing it all was, and when one tried to straighten things out in one's mind afterwards, one couldn't always disentangle what one definitely saw from what one thought one might have seen. You do understand, don't you?' Manton groaned inwardly. Clearly she was an old girl with one of those vivid imaginations that helped her to give as definite facts things that she had imagined had happened, or ought to have happened. There was not an officer at the Yard who didn't know the type and yet there was always the lay public who thought direct testimony must always be much stronger than circumstantial evidence. Miss Fenwick-Blunt sailed imperturbably on. 'I think I know who dropped the pistol on to the floor. Of course I can't say that I saw him actually throw it down, but looking back on it, I don't think that anyone else but this man could have done it.'

'And who was the man?' asked Manton quietly.

'Oh, the warder who was just behind Mr. Tarrant when he was killed. I'm afraid I don't know his name.'

'Why do you say this?'

'Well, just immediately after the shot, I saw this warder person put his right hand straight down his side. Of course I couldn't see if he had anything in his hand but almost at once I heard something fall on the floor; and the pistol was found just there, wasn't it?' she concluded with a note of triumph in her voice.

'Why didn't you tell us this before?' asked Manton.

'I've told you, Inspector; it was only when I started to think about it afterwards that I was sure that this was what had happened. You know the way things suddenly come back to you', she added hopefully.

Manton leaned forward in his chair and suddenly said, 'Where have you been all the afternoon and evening before coming along here?'

If he expected Miss Blunt to be surprised at this sudden question, he was disappointed. She just gave him a quizzical little smile and replied: 'Oh, I left my hotel about six o'clock and I've been out since. I went to the Rex Cinema in Piccadilly and only came out of there about ten o'clock.' She went on brightly: 'I'm afraid I can't tell you much about the film. You see, I went hoping it would take my mind off all this, but instead I found myself hardly noticing the screen but thinking more and more about the murder.' With a twinkle she added: 'I haven't been drinking if that's what you're worrying about, Inspector.'

That had been part of the reason for Manton's question and he smiled at her challenge.

'Well, thank you, Miss Blunt, for coming along. We'll remember what you said. I must say I don't see a warder choosing the Court as the best place to get rid of a prisoner: even assuming he had some reason for wanting to do so.'

He got up and spoke to Talper who was playing his usual silent rôle.

'See Miss Blunt out, would you, Sergeant?' He looked at his watch. 'You'd better send her back in my car; it's not very easy to get a cab at this hour.'

And so Miss Fenwick-Blunt departed as calm and urbane as when she had arrived.

Alone in his office, Manton slowly shook his head and rubbed his chin. Then he took a piece of paper and in apparent deep contemplation wrote:

Suspects :
First Choice - Pinty
Second Choice - Glindy
Hartman
MacBruce
Miss F. Blunt

Beneath the list of names, he added: 'But why **any** of them?—in this case find a motive, find the murderer.'

Chapter Ten

Mrs. Longbucket, who was the good lady who owned and controlled with an iron hand the boarding-house where Jakes Hartman had a room, had had considerable experience in that particular line of business. In fact to hear her talk, one got the impression that she was descended from a long line of highly respectable Bayswater boarding-house proprietresses, and undoubtedly, to give her her due (which she constantly complained her lodgers never did), there was little she didn't know about running a boarding-house. That is far from saying that she always had a house full of beaming, satisfied guests. Probably not even the most perfect paragon amongst boarding-house proprietors could boast that.

Now Mrs. Longbucket had fixed ideas and implacable rules which she considered necessary, not of course for the comfort and welfare of the inmates, but for the maintenance of a good time and a respectable house. When you had some of these strange foreign gentlemen in your house, you couldn't afford to have the sort of *laissez-faire* atmosphere which they usually brought with them. So it was that one of her most rigid and unswerving rules dealt with the question of her male guests entertaining their lady friends in the house. Briefly the position was this. Provided adequate notice was given, there was no objection to their being brought in for dinner, but it was expected that they would be introduced to everyone at the table and any sitting together at the far end was heavily frowned upon. Afterwards the awkward young couple could sit on in the dining-room until they wished to leave the house. On no account, however, was a visitor allowed to go up to the bedrooms, and an infringement of this rule led to an immediate and frigid request to the inmate to pay his bill and seek his bed elsewhere. Only in this way, felt Mrs. Long-bucket, could her respectable name be maintained.

On this particular evening she had just got into bed when the front-door bell rang. As she crossly clambered out and put on her dressing-gown, she wondered who on earth it could be at such an hour of the night. In fact, it was only just after eleven but everyone was in their room and half an hour before, she had locked up down-stairs and turned off the lights. Like most ladies of her age and brand, she looked a very odd sight when roused from her bed in the middle of the night. Her hair could hardly be seen for steel curlers, her dressing-gown was of customary red flannel and her expression was a mixture of annoyance and trepidation. Annoyance, of course, at being got up in this fashion, and trepidation because she never imagined that anyone who knocked on her respectable door after bedtime could be up to any good. She descended the stairs, and mentally pre-pared herself to resist an assault on her virtue by one of the lustful creatures she envisaged as haunting the streets of London at this hour of the night.

There were two bolts, a chain and a mortice lock to be dealt with before she could operate the yale lock and open the door a fraction to peer out at the unwel-come caller.

Maisie Jenks had never met Mrs. Longbucket, though she'd heard a great deal about her; but the

latter had never heard of Maisie, for Jakes had steadfastly refused to invite her to the house because of the
existing rules for lady visitors. What Mrs. Longbucket
saw as she peered out was a rather pretty girl of about
twenty, wearing a heather mixture coloured overcoat
and carrying a small light suitcase in her hand. Anticipating the question, she said in a distinctly disapproving voice: 'I'm afraid I've no rooms to let at all', and
was just about to shut the door and go through all the
business with the locks and bolts again, when the girl
spoke in a quiet but urgent tone.

'I've called to see Mr. Hartman. Would you please
let me in and tell him I'm here?' Mrs. Longbucket
made no effort to admit her, and Maisie went on: 'It's
frightfully important, I must see him at once. Please let
me in.'

'He's in bed and probably asleep', said Mrs. Longbucket, playing for time.

'It's terribly urgent, Mrs. Longbucket, I promise you
I wouldn't have dreamed of coming at this hour if it
wasn't. I simply must see him to-night.'

Mrs. Longbucket's hostility was slightly mitigated by
the fact that Maisie knew her name; and she could see
that the girl was nearly at the end of her tether, and was
keeping her emotions under control only with a considerable effort. Grudgingly, however, she opened the
door fully and Maisie Jenks stepped into the hall. Mrs.
Longbucket shut the door and led the way into the
dining-room where she switched on the light.

'You'd better wait in here while I go and see if he'll
come down.'

And with that somewhat ungracious remark, she left
the room and started mounting the creaking stairs. It

was typical of her attitude towards her midnight caller that she never bothered to inquire her name before going up to Jakes' room.

Maisie looked round the room and shivered. It was ghastly in its Victorianism and an ancient smell of boiled cabbage hung about like a pall of poison gas.

She took off her gloves and sat on the edge of the table. She'd long since decided just how she was going to approach the matter that had brought her so unexpectedly to Bayswater. Upstairs a door closed and she heard footsteps coming down the stairs. A moment later Jakes in his dressing-gown and with hair on end, walked into the room, looking as though he'd just received news that he'd become the father of triplets.

'Hello, Jakes!'

Maisie realized it was an inadequate greeting for the occasion but could think of none more suitable at that moment. The person to whom she addressed it was still visibly trying to gather his wits together. To say the least, it was a bit of a shock to be awakened out of a particularly deep sleep and told that a girl wanted you downstairs in the dining-room, and would you please go and show her the way out as soon as possible. Jakes continued to look as bemused and inarticulate as Tristan after drinking the love potion, but eventually he found his voice.

'What on earth has happened, Maisie? Why have you come here at this hour?' Although in his heart of hearts, Jakes knew quite well that this was no normal visit, he somehow longed to hear her reply airily that she had just thought she'd look in as she was going past on her way home from a party. At that moment his gaze fell upon the small suitcase which was beside her on one of the dining-room chairs. 'And you've got your case too. Darling, what's the matter?'

It flashed through Jakes' mind that Maisie must have committed the murder and was now running away from the police. Her reply to his anxious queries was hardly calculated to calm his mind.

'Jakes, dear, please don't ask me any questions because I just daren't . . . can't answer them. I've left home and I'm not going back. I've nowhere to go and simply had to come to someone who'd help me.'

At this last pathetic little plea, the manly side of Jakes took over from the agitated goggler.

'Of course I'll help you, darling, but you must tell me what's happened', and he moved over to Maisie to give practical expression to his words.

'I'm just terribly confused and rather frightened but I can't tell you any more . . . it's all so incredible and terrifying.'

Maisie shuddered and started to cry, gently at first, but then with great silent sobs. Jakes held her tightly to him as she rested her head on his shoulder and gave herself up to uncontrollable tears. For a time they stayed like that, with him gently stroking her pretty head and whispering soft words of comfort into her ear, as one might with a child who has just suffered an inconsolable disappointment. Eventually she regained control of her emotions and after wiping her eyes and blowing her nose spoke in quite a steady voice.

'I must look a frightful sight. I'm sorry, Jakes, but I feel better now and it's such a relief to be with you. I realize how impossible I'm being in not telling you anything.'

'It's not that,' said Jakes, 'but unless I know what's wrong, I can't help you as well as I could otherwise. Don't you see, darling, you really ought to tell me, so that we can decide together what's the best thing to do. It must be something pretty serious to have brought you here at this hour.'

It was perhaps as well that Jakes was sitting down to receive Maisie's next remark. In a serious voice now quite under control again, she said: 'Can we go away— right away—together? Perhaps even get married?' Then almost as an afterthought: 'You do want to marry me, don't you, Jakes?'

Up until an hour before there had been nothing he wanted to do more and the prospect then seemed hopelessly out of reach. Now, here was his loved one, whom he'd only dared to kiss for the first time a few days before, suggesting that they go away and get married. In none of his many day dreams had he foreseen things turning out like this and it was perhaps scarcely surprising that he didn't react with the enthusiastic alacrity which he might have shown in other circumstances.

Maisie looked on the verge of tears again.

'Please, please, Jakes, take me away', she said with such urgency that he was galvanized into action at last. He got up as if to leave the room. 'Where are you going?'

'I'll go and find old dragon Longbucket and tell her you're stopping the night here.'

'Oh no, Jakes, I can't spend a night here. Can't we leave at once? Oh, I know it sounds fantastic and that it's asking an awful lot. But—but this is one of the first places they'll start looking for me when they discover that I've left home.'

'All right, I'll go and put a few things in a bag and then we'll buzz off.'

Jakes gave her a comforting smile as he said this and left the room to go up to his bedroom. He felt far from composed, however, as he tiptoed about his room wondering what he should pack and how he should break his departure to Mrs. Longbucket. It would all be much easier, he reflected, if he knew just what was in store for them, or even if he only had an idea as to what they were going to do when they stepped outside the front door.

Ten minutes later he rejoined Maisie in the still aromatic dining-room. He was wearing a greatcoat over the working suit he'd put on, and he carried a small overnight bag in his right hand. On the hall table he left an envelope addressed to Mrs. Longbucket. It contained a brief note explaining that owing to family illness he had had to leave suddenly, but that he expected to be back in a day or so. He knew Mrs. Longbucket wouldn't be taken in for a moment by the family sickness business, but it was the best he could think of at the time—in fact the only thing. As to the second part, he secretly doubted whether he would be back in a day or so. It seemed that the die was being truly cast and that Jakes Hartman had reached a turning point in his life. Thus it was that Maisie and he quietly left the sleeping house and walked away down the dimly lit street. A church clock struck a quarter to one as they turned the corner at the end of the road and disappeared from view.

Chapter Eleven

THE next day Manton spent waiting hourly for news of Pinty. The whole nation had become Pinty conscious overnight and it seemed impossible that the day could go by without news of him coming in from some quarter. But as it wore on and Manton went over the known facts for the hundredth time hoping against hope to be confronted by some obvious simple circumstance which he had previously either failed to notice, or more likely had been trying to fit into the wrong place in the puzzle, and still no news came in, he began to feel frustrated to a degree he had never before experienced on a case.

After a further interview with Mrs. Pinty, he was more than ever satisfied that she had no part in the mystery, but equally it was clear that she had only a sketchy idea of her husband's background. She had supplied the police with the addresses of relatives with whom he might have made some contact, but needless to say he had not done so.

Manton thought it very possible from his police experience of outwardly placid suburban life that Mr. Pinty had another establishment somewhere, and that he was now in safe hiding, with a discreet and loyal second 'Mrs. Pinty' looking after him. It was always the most respectable little men who had these second wives tucked safely away, unknown to and unsuspected by their own families and their friends at the Bowling

Club. And for that reason, it was always the very devil to track them down.

After lunch he decided to go down to the Old Bailey again. He hadn't been there since leaving the previous morning after the murder, and it was only because he couldn't think of anything better to do that he decided to revisit the scene of the crime. Resourceful though he was, he had by now made up his mind that his investigation couldn't be carried forward a single inch until Pinty was found. He was almost certainly the murderer. He'd probably had a sudden brainstorm listening to Sir Genser and pulled out a gun to shoot Tarrant and so end the trial. So ran Manton's somewhat flippant thoughts as he rode eastwards to the Court. And, of course, foreseeing the possibility of being driven beyond endurance by the Old Fake, Pinty had conveniently brought his Luger to Court with him. Manton dismissed these light ideas from his mind and concentrated once more on the cold hard facts to see if there were any further deductions to be drawn which he hadn't already got in mind. It was clear that Pinty, or whoever the murderer was, had come to Court that morning with deliberate murder in his heart. And not only that, but he or she was prepared to take a gigantic risk in putting his or her plan into execution. Obviously from the fact that such a fearfully risky setting was chosen for the crime, one could deduce that the murderer was working against time; it must have been a question of then or never. But why should anyone want to murder a man when the odds were that the State would accomplish the task legally for him if he cared to wait but a few weeks? Again the answer to that must be that the murderer couldn't wait that length of time and had to act with dramatic suddenness and run the risk of almost certain and immediate arrest. But was it perhaps such an incredible and outside chance that the murderer had so far eluded them? Maybe it hadn't been from his point of view such a big risk as it had appeared to others to be. After all—the fact was that he was still at large. As these thoughts chased after each other through his mind, another one suddenly intruded. What if the murderer had not meant to kill Tarrant at all and his bullet was intended for someone else? But if this was so, why choose that setting and that particular moment to pull the trigger? And if Tarrant wasn't the intended victim, then who was?

By the time his car pulled up outside the Old Bailey, Manton had rejected that idea and was once more back where he'd started—namely that the answer to all these questions lay with Pinty. Never had there been such a case in which motive was not only the vital clue but, as it seemed at the moment, the only clue—and a missing one at that.

Since the murder, Number One Court had not been used at all and as Manton entered he felt he was almost intruding on a secret tête-à-tête of the walls—walls which had borne silent witness of so many life and death struggles and had seen the basest human motives exposed before them. He walked slowly and thoughtfully across the empty Court, his footsteps breaking the air of silent conspiracy. When he got to the jury box, he sat down in the seat which had last been occupied by John Pinty. He gazed at the empty seats in front of him and once more saw them filled with tense expectant faces as they had been on the day of Tarrant's death.

From his pocket he took out his pipe and holding it in his left hand as an imaginary revolver, shot an imaginary Tarrant through the heart. Having satisfied himself of what he already knew, he moved back to the seat behind, which had been occupied by Miss Fenwick-Blunt. Again he repeated the performance. 'Yes, that's possible all right,' he murmured to himself, 'though if that old dragon fired the shot, it must have almost shattered Pinty's left eardrum. Perhaps that's why he took to flight.' Next he went down to the lowest floor level and sat in MacBruce's seat. Not so easy from here, though of course Tarrant was turning to his left, that is towards MacBruce when he met his death.

Manton made a mental note to look up MacBruce's record of service when he got back to the Yard. There was something odd about that chap which went beyond normal Scottish dourness. As he moved across and sat down in Jakes Hartman's seat, he came to the conclusion that it was even less likely that the latter had committed the murder. Anyway, why should he want to kill Tarrant? Back to the original question again. It mattered not which way he set out on this problem, he always came back to that nagging and unanswerable question.

Finally he went up to where Maisie Jenks had sat and looked across at the jury box. She certainly had had a perfect view of the scene from there, and she had clearly seen something that made her scream and apparently go off into a genuine faint. So far as we know, thought Manton, the only person she knew in that part of the Court was the shorthand writer and therefore it seems reasonable to suppose that it was some action of his that caused her to react as she did. What action? Why,

the drawing of a pistol preparatory to shooting Tarrant
—too easy! Yes, a jolly sight too easy, he reflected
savagely; but it was something to bear in mind and
certainly it was simple enough to be the truth. Suddenly
he sat up and spoke aloud: 'Yes and now she's disappeared; and I bet she's gone off with Hartman! That
links up and makes sense.'

When he left the Court, Simon Manton was not at all
sure that he wasn't still chasing his own tail but one or
two bits of the puzzle now seemed to be in their right
places and a more definite idea was beginning to take
shape in his head.

And while everyone read about Mr. Pinty in their
papers, talked about him as they ate their meals, and
scanned their neighbours' faces in the hope of recogniz-
ing him, he, unhappy man, lay unceremoniously in
some bushes with a bullet through his head.

Chapter Twelve

THE next morning just as Manton was about to leave his home for the Yard, the telephone bell rang.

'Is that Chief Inspector Manton's home?' a male voice asked.

'Yes, Manton speaking.'

'Oh, sir, this is Boland Road Police Station, Detective Sergeant Saintley speaking. I was given your home number by the Yard. Pinty has been found dead up on Hampstead Heath.'

The sergeant's voice vibrated with excitement. There was a pause before Manton replied, and he found himself quivering with hopeful excitement as he gave the necessary instructions over the wire and then dashed out to his car.

'Boland Road Police Station, and step on it, Harry', he said to his driver as he flung himself into a back seat.

Sergeant Saintley was a wise young officer. He had detected from a note in Manton's voice that he was pretty much on edge, and in these circumstances he arranged everything so that he could go on straight to where Pinty's body had been found, without hanging about at the Station.

It was about twenty-five minutes after the call that Manton's car lurched round the bend from the main road and pulled up outside the Police Station. Before he had time to get out, a head popped through the window.

'I'm Saintley, sir. I expect you'd like to go to the

scene at once, and we can get out there straight away.'

'Fine,' replied Manton, 'jump in. You direct my driver.'

On the way up to the Heath, Sergeant Saintley told him how Pinty's body had been found early that morning in a thicket on the north-east side of the Heath. A well-known local scamp, who apparently lived rough up on the Heath and spent his days begging in the streets with a large brass plate labelled 'Blind' around his neck and a pitiful-looking mongrel squatting abjectly beside him, had made the discovery. In fact, neither the vagrant nor his dog, were the sorry-looking figures they made themselves out to be, as was shown by the fact that the former had lost no time in claiming a reward and showing a marked disinclination to assist when told there wasn't one. It appeared that the hound was wont to get up before his master, and do a preliminary roam around before the latter rose from mother earth and shook off the leaves, after which he was as ready to face the new day as his dog. No time had to be wasted on such refinements as washing, shaving or even dressing. On this particular morning, Guido, the tramp (no one knew why he went by a respectable Italian name when he'd never been closer to the Mediterranean than Tottenham Court Road) had been awakened about six o'clock by Gravy, the hapless hound, barking his ugly head off. Guido had hurled a few of his own oaths in the direction of the noise but these only seemed to make Gravy redouble his efforts to disturb the early morning peace of the Heath. At last Guido got up, shook off a few leaves and ambled off in the direction of the barks. There was an early morning mist and he stumbled over the ground. About forty yards from where he'd been sleeping, he found Gravy leaping about inside a small thicket of blackberry bushes and, if anything, barking more furiously than before. The tramp had no desire to penetrate the thorny patch in order to see what was the dog's interest there, and at first he tried to entice Gravy out. But without avail, and finally wrapping his fourth and top overcoat well around him, he waded in. There in the centre he found a man lying on his back. It didn't take him long to see that this was no sleeping fellow-traveller, apart from the unlikely choice of such a bed, but a man with a gaping wound in his head.

Guido had got out of it as soon as possible, and about thirty minutes later had arrived at Boland Road Police Station.

By the time Detective Sergeant Saintley had given Manton Guido's story in its broad outline, they had arrived at the scene, and the two C.I.D. men got out. A police cordon had been thrown around the spot to keep out the interested gazes of those whose curiosity was greater than their discretion. Several press men gathered round Manton as he slammed the car door behind him. He gave them a friendly smile.

'Sorry boys—nothing doing', he said firmly.

'Can't you give us a break at all, Inspector? Remember the mid-day editions.'

Another broke in: 'Is it true it's Pinty's body you've got your chaps guarding up here like the Crown jewels?'

Manton smiled at the questioner. He got on well with the newspaper men and so far he'd never been let down by any of them.

'Sorry. I think "no comment" is the recognized formula, isn't it?' he said.

He pushed through them followed by Saintley who led the way over to the thicket where the body was. Poor little Mr. Pinty presented an incongruous sight. His eyes were closed and his hair on one side was falling untidily across his brow. His mouth was open and except that he was dead and not snoring, he might have been fast asleep. The brambles around the body had been pressed back so often in the last hour or so that they now offered no resistance to the curious onlooker. Just behind Mr. Pinty's head was his black homburg hat and he still had on his overcoat which was buttoned up. Manton knelt down beside the body and examined it with interest. There was a neat round hole in the right temple and a much less neat wound at the left side of the head where it was obvious that the bullet had come out. To his practised eye it appeared that there were scorch marks by the entrance wound but scientific examination would later confirm this or not as the case might be. Gently Manton put both his hands beneath the body and slowly turned it on to its side.

'Here, Sergeant, get a handkerchief and fish this out.' Sergeant Saintley knelt beside the Inspector and picked up from the ground a .38 revolver which had previously been hidden beneath Pinty's body.

Manton stood up and holding out his own handkerchief took the weapon from the other man.

'We'd better not play about with this too much. Let's hope that under scientific examination it'll have a story to tell us.' He handed it to a junior officer who was standing nearby and once more bent down over the corpse. 'Anyone been through the pockets yet?'

Sergeant Saintley answered.

'Yes, sir, when I first came up, I did a superficial check, but after I'd established identity I didn't bother any further.'

'Well we'd better have a look now.'

Carefully Manton slid his hand into the greatcoat pockets. From these he produced an old fourpenny bus ticket, a season ticket on the tube between Pinty's home and his office in the City, and one glove, the right one. For a moment he wondered at the significance of this until he noticed that Mr. Pinty had apparently died with his left one still on his hand.

He next unbuttoned the greatcoat and equally methodically started extracting things from the pockets of Mr. Pinty's best blue suit. They were chiefly the common, everyday objects that men cram into their pockets to the pained remonstrance of their tailors. A pipe with a well-chewed stem, a tobacco pouch, a cheap self-propelling pencil, a lighter as well as a box of matches and a small bunch of keys. From the breast pocket he pulled out a clean, neatly folded handkerchief. He was just beginning to reflect that the finding of Mr. Pinty didn't look as though it were going to be a solution in itself, when his exploring fingers felt a folded sheet of paper in the inside pocket. He removed it and unfolded it before the interested gaze of his subordinates. It was headed *H.M. Prison, Brixton* and one glance was enough to show him that it was a letter from Tarrant. Manton's pulse quickened with excitement as he scanned this unexpected find. It was dated two days before the trial and read as follows:

You and I both know what I mean when I say I can see only one way out of this for me. Sorry, but I'm more interested in my own neck than other people's at the moment, so that's the way it's probably got to be, *unless* you care to put matters right in the next twenty-four hours.'

Manton carefully folded the note again and placed it in his pocket.

'Wonder where the envelope has got to?' he said aloud but speaking to himself. With a thoughtful frown he turned to Sergeant Saintley. 'When the photographer has done his stuff, get the body to the mortuary and I'll get hold of Dr. Craig to arrange the post mortem and notify the Coroner.'

He turned to leave the scene and Saintley, after a hurried word to his assistants, followed. Before he had time to say anything, Manton spoke.

'What's your view of it?' and he turned the full gaze of his bright blue eyes on to the Sergeant.

'Well, sir, there are one or two things which strike me as odd. At first sight it appears to be obvious murder. Body found hidden in a thicket on one of the less frequented parts of the Heath, and it's only two days later that it's discovered and it might very well have been longer still. But if it was murder, sir, how did the murderer get his intended victim into the middle of a place like that before shooting him? He or she could hardly have said: "Look here, I'm proposing to murder you but would you first mind coming over to this lonely bush so that nobody will see or hear me do it." '

Manton smiled and broke in: 'But he could have been murdered elsewhere and then dumped where we found him.'

'Yes, I've thought of that too, sir. But again it's curious, if that happened, that we haven't found any marks of a body being draggged to the spot. After all, it's quite a little way from the road and I should have expected to find some marks, especially as the ground is not all that hard at the moment. But I've looked carefully and there aren't any such marks, sir.'

Manton nodded appreciatively; he too had looked for signs indicating that the body had been dragged to its hiding place, and had failed to find any. It could of course have been carried there; but dead bodies, even of small men, are an infernal weight.

Sergeant Saintley now warmed to his subject, and anxious to impress his superior officer, went on: 'Well then, sir, there's the suicide aspect, and it seems to me at the moment as if that's the better bet. In fact there's only one snag about that. Why should anyone stage his own death inside a beastly thicket of brambles where no one was likely to find him for some time? Usually it seems to me that most of these suicide Johnnies are exhibitionists and like to stage an act accordingly.'

He looked at Manton to see how he was reacting to all these reconstruction theories. The latter spoke half-musingly to himself when at last he did give tongue.

'Suicide is certainly very much a possibility and, maybe, one might say a probability. There was something between Pinty and Tarrant, that's clear from the note we've just found and we shall have to find out exactly what lies behind it. Anyway, assume for the moment that Pinty is driven to kill Tarrant in such a way that it is clear to him that he cannot possibly get away with it. In those circumstances and having achieved his object, he decides to kill himself. In fact he almost certainly had it all worked out beforehand. I agree that for the moment I don't see why he should have chosen this particular place for self-immolation, but he did and that's that.'

Saintley nodded wisely and wished he knew what self-immolation meant. Anyway, it sounded a good word to remember and stick in his next report.

'Well I'll get back to Boland Road now', said Manton coming out of his day dream of reconstruction. 'I'd like to have a word with this Guido, myself. You stay up here till everything's cleared up, will you?'

He managed to get to his car and drive away before the alert press had time to ask any more questions.

At the Police Station, Manton found Sergeant Talper who had arrived there a few minutes before. He was cursing himself and others unnamed that he hadn't got there earlier to be at his chief's side. However, Manton soon mollified him and told him of the morning's discovery.

'I'm not sure, Andy, that there's very much more we can do up here and I think we'd best get back to the Yard and start operations from there. While we're waiting for the experts' reports to come in, we might have Glindy along and see what he can tell us about the letter.'

Chapter Thirteen

IT was just before noon when the car bearing the two officers swung off the Embankment and came to a halt. Manton quickly made his way to his office while Sergeant Talper looked into the Central Office to collect any messages that might have come in. Shortly after he joined Manton in his room and gave him the sheet of paper which he was holding in his right hand.

'This seems to be all.'

It was a message to the effect that a Mrs. Longbucket had made a long and indignant phone call to the Yard. She had read all about the Tarrant murder in the papers and now wished to report that her lodger, Mr. Hartman, had mysteriously decamped in the middle of the night after receiving a call from a young woman. From descriptions which she had read, Mrs. Long-bucket was quite certain that she was the missing Maisie Jenks. The message finished by saying that Mrs. Long-bucket had a good name and didn't wish to get mixed up in such goings on and that it was the first and last time she'd ever have a murderer under her roof.

'She seems to have jumped to conclusions', murmured Manton. 'We must find those two, nevertheless. There's a lot that girl has got to explain.'

There was a knock on the door and Prison Officer Albert Glindy was ushered in. Simon Manton smiled at the warder and got the immediate impression that he was in an extremely nervous state. His somewhat pointed face was whiter than usual and his mouth was set in a firm line. He sat down in the proffered chair and replied to the Inspector's greeting with a bare nod of the head.

Manton started speaking as soon as all three of them were seated.

'I believe you saw a certain amount of Tarrant before the trial, didn't you?'

'Not a great deal. He was in the prison hospital like they always are awaiting trial.'

'Know whether he wrote many letters while he was waiting?'

'Some.'

'Not very chatty, are you?' said Manton, who was getting rather tired of prodding witnesses who shouldn't have needed such treatment.

'Well, I told you, I wasn't in charge of him while he was awaiting trial. I don't know about his letters. They're allowed to write as many as they like at that stage, of course.'

Slowly Manton withdrew from his pocket the note which had been found on Pinty a few hours before. With equally slow deliberation, he unfolded it and passed it across the table to the watchful Glindy.

'Just read that, will you? That note was found on the dead body of Pinty, the juror; the man who took a powder after the shooting in Court the other day.' He paused while the warder carefully read the short but cryptic missive. 'Ever seen it before?'

Glindy looked up and straight into Manton's eyes before answering.

'No, I haven't ever seen it before.'

'I thought perhaps you might be able to help me about how Tarrant came to write it.'

'I'm afraid I can't.'

Manton looked at the white face across the table and it was with great seriousness when he spoke again.

'I'm sure you want to help as much as you can and I'd be glad if you would bear in mind that you and I are both on the same side. Now, did Tarrant ever say anything to you about his case? Did he ever discuss its possibilities with you?'

'No. He was always pretty cagey about what he'd done and how he, of all people, came to be involved in a murder. He did say once or twice that he'd got to make up his mind just how he was going to handle the matter when the trial started, but he never told me what he meant.' Now that Glindy had started talking, he was doing so quite naturally, as if he had suddenly decided that it was a safe thing to do. 'He seemed to enjoy talking about sport and things of general interest like that. But about his case—no. And it wasn't for me to question him either.'

Glindy stopped almost as suddenly as he'd started, and for a time all was silent save for the rain which beat against the windows in a sudden November storm.

Manton was the next to speak and he did so in almost casual tones.

'Did you have any reason to kill Tarrant?'

The words fell from his lips and were followed by a tense silence. Manton gazed fixedly at the warder who seemed to be seeking inspiration from the streaming windows and Talper took in the whole scene rather like a cat waiting for something to happen.

Glindy turned his gaze from the windows back to

Manton and said quite quietly: 'You said just now that we were on the same side. Are you suggesting I committed the murder?'

'I also said just now, Glindy, that I didn't think you were being as helpful as you might be and certainly not as helpful as one would expect a prison officer to be in the circumstances. No, I'm not accusing you of murder, but if I happen to draw any false conclusions, it'll be entirely your own fault.' There was another fateful pause and Manton continued: 'You must admit that it's extremely difficult for anyone to believe that you were within a foot of Tarrant when he was shot and that yet you have no idea who fired the shot. And then you quickly disappear from the scene because you say you felt sick. If any story is likely to cover its author in suspicion, that one is. Just think about it yourself for a moment.'

But Glindy's talking mood, such as it had been, was now over and he only sat glowering with that frightened look about him which Manton had noticed when he first entered the room.

'I can't tell you any more than I have already; and if you think you've got enough evidence to charge me with murder, you'd better go ahead and do it.' His tone was challenging.

Manton got up.

'O.K. I'll let you know when I want to see you again.' With that Albert Glindy left the room to return to Brixton whence he came. 'What do you make of him now, Andy? It seems to me there are too many people in this case covering up and acting suspiciously. They presumably can't all be murderers, and if not, why the hell don't they co-operate?'

Sergeant Talper rubbed his lower lip with his pencil, and spoke thoughtfully.

'Of course that old girl, Mrs. Blunt-Fanshaw or whatever her silly name is, said she thought it was Glindy who dropped the revolver after the murder. If that's true, it means of course that he and no one else is the murderer.'

'And what about Pinty and this morning's find?' said Manton quizzically.

Chapter Fourteen

IT was shortly after lunch that Manton decided to do a round of the experts to see what they could tell him about the body and the pistol which they'd been examining. He got up from his desk, reached for his hat and coat and was about to open the door when there was a perfunctory knock on it, and in walked Inspector MacBruce. He held a mid-day edition of one of the evening papers in his hand and his tone was almost triumphant.

'What did I tell you, Manton? Find Pinty and you've solved your crime.'

'I wasn't aware it was solved', replied Manton somewhat dryly.

The other looked astonished for a moment.

'Don't tell me, man, that you still have doubts about who shot Tarrant. Isn't it now as clear as daylight?'

'Go on, let's have your theory', said Manton without much enthusiasm.

'Well, of course, Pinty shot Tarrant because Tarrant was going to disclose something about him in the witness box—I know that'll need a bit of tidying up—and then realizing that, though he'd sealed Tarrant's lips, he hadn't left himself an escape hole, he committed suicide as being a better way out than judicial hanging.'

'I agree,' said Manton, 'that that all fits up to a point, but it still leaves all sorts of things unexplained. For instance why kill yourself in a place where you're not likely to be found for some time?'

But MacBruce was not to be put off by details of that sort.

'That's something you plain-clothes folk are paid extra to find out', he said.

Manton looked thoughtfully at his visitor and with a half-smile said: 'Well, thanks for your theory; and now let's hear what really brought you here. I'm sure it wasn't just to tell me what you've read in the papers and to air your latest theories.'

MacBruce might have smiled but didn't.

'I happened to be up at the Yard and thought I'd drop in and see how things were when I'd finished my other business.' He paused and Manton waited for him to go on. 'I see a .38 revolver was found by his body. Been able to trace that yet?'

'Is that in the paper too?' asked Manton surprised.

For a moment MacBruce appeared a trifle flustered.

'Er—no—I heard that in the building; general talk you know. But have you been able to trace it?'

Now why the devil is he so interested in whether I've traced the revolver, thought Manton, when he's equally determined to sell me his theory of the crime in which it doesn't matter a damn whether the revolver belonged to Pinty or Al Capone? Aloud he said: 'I think it may have belonged to Hartman, the shorthand writer', and watched the other's reaction.

For a moment MacBruce looked thoughtfully puzzled. He was about to say something but seemed suddenly to change his mind. Eventually he looked at Manton and spoke again.

'If you think Hartman murdered Tarrant and Pinty, why don't you arrest him?'

'I didn't say I did think so, and in any event, he's

disappeared with his girl friend—the one whose scream was such a useful distraction to the murderer. Anyway I should have thought you'd have read all about it in your paper.'

MacBruce glared and turned to go as Sergeant Talper entered the room. They passed and the door closed between them.

'What did he want?' asked Talper.

'Oh, just fishing', said Manton pleasantly. 'I think we'll make a few inquiries about our friend, MacBruce. Come on, Andy, let's first go and see these experts.'

Chapter Fifteen

THE rain had ceased as they drove out on to the Embankment but there appeared to be every likelihood of the fog coming down again at nightfall.

When they got to the mortuary, Dr. Craig was just about to leave. He seemed pleased to see Manton and the three men went into the office to exchange ideas. It was a small room with a large table and a huge fire which made the thermometer register tropical heat. There were just sufficient chairs and the men sat down delighted to enjoy the warmth, each wondering how long he could conscientiously remain there.

The doctor was the first to speak. He was in his mid-forties and a tubby little man with a red face and a mass of cropped black hair which stood out from his head like a sort of pallisade. He was regarded as one of the ablest pathologists in the land and he always got on well with the police officers with whom he worked. He and Manton had been on several cases together and each had considerable respect for the opinion of the other.

When they were all seated, Dr. Craig said: 'Well, Inspector, I don't know whether I'm going to be able to tell you very much that'll lighten your task. It seems to me you've got a real tricky customer on your hands— if it's murder.'

'You rule out suicide then?' said Manton.

'Not entirely. But I was up at the scene shortly after you left this morning and before they'd moved the body, and personally I don't think he'd have fallen quite like that if he'd stood in that bramble place and blown his brains out. He could have, mind you, and I should have to admit as much in cross-examination, but somehow it didn't satisfy me as genuine suicide. Apart, of course, from the fact that I can't see why anyone should want to choose that place to commit self-murder.'

Manton smiled. 'I know,' he said, 'everyone says that of course and it is a factor against the suicide theory. But I expect you also appreciate, Doctor, that there were no dragging marks, such as one would have expected to find if a body had been hauled across the ground and dumped.'

The doctor nodded.

'Yes—your Sergeant up there told me that when I asked him about it.'

'What about scorch marks?' asked Manton, changing the subject.

'Yes, I expect you saw them round the entrance wound. And that of course means that if it was murder, the weapon was held surprisingly close to the victim's head.'

'How long do you estimate that he'd been dead?'

The doctor pursed his lips.

'Not easy to say with any certainty. Round about forty-eight hours, and I should say *in situ* for about the same period.'

Manton nodded thoughtfully.

'Yes, of course, forty-eight hours back from this morning brings us to the time Tarrant was shot and Pinty disappeared. I gather you think he was dumped there very soon after death—if it was murder, that is?'

It was the doctor's turn to nod.

'If it was suicide, he apparently removed his right glove to do it and in that event, you may get some fingerprints from the gun.'

'We may,' said Manton, 'and I think if that's all you can tell us from your angle, we'll go and find out about that straight away.'

Silence reigned while each tried to summon up sufficient will-power to leave the friendly warmth of the room. Suddenly the phone rang. Manton lifted the receiver.

'Yes, speaking.'

Thereafter there was more silence, interrupted only by Manton's monosyllabic interjections as he listened with growing interest to his caller. At last with a word of thanks, he rang off and stood up.

'That was the laboratory on the phone. They've examined the gun and found one of Pinty's prints on it. There was an empty case in the chamber but no live rounds in the magazine. As I thought, it's a .38 Smith and Wesson army-type issue.' The other two men remained silent and Manton went on: 'Of course that's a fairly common type of revolver; but it's also the same sort that P.C. Moss was shot with, and in his case we've never found the weapon. The lab say they may be able to let us know something further later on.'

Chapter Sixteen

THE next day a watery sun peered without enthusiasm from the November sky, but did little to mitigate the effects of an east wind which seemed to be blowing straight up the river. It was shortly after eleven o'clock, and Manton had just returned to his room following a summons to the Assistant Commissioner's office where he'd been required to bring that illustrious man up to date on the Tarrant-Pinty murders. Unfortunately for him, though hardly surprisingly in the circumstances, the two murders had received and were still receiving an almost unprecedented amount of space in the columns of the daily press.

The majority of the papers, and certainly those which fed the voracious public with the more spectacular aspects of the case, had adopted the MacBruce theory. Namely that for some reason, which they urged the police to discover and reveal, Pinty had murdered Tarrant in Court and then committed suicide by blowing his brains out. Though it had not been possible to keep the news of the discovery of Pinty's body from the press, Manton had taken what steps he could to see that none of the details should leak out, and he reflected that the suicide story might not in fact be a bad thing in the long run as it might induce a sense of false security in the murderer's mind—provided always of course that it was murder. In the circumstances, Manton felt bound to work on that assumption since, so far, he was unable to exclude it. One newspaper, however, noted for its lurid reporting, had openly told its readers that the police now had a double murder on their hands and that sensational developments might be expected almost hourly. Manton had been amused to see that one of the other daily papers, not far behind the first in its colourful reporting, had primly taken the latter to task for pandering, without foundation, to the baser but nevertheless natural instincts of its readers.

He opened a drawer at the side of his desk and pulled out a clean sheet of foolscap paper which he placed before him. He then got up and with thoughtful deliberation sharpened a pencil. This done, he laid the pencil on the paper and sat down again. To those who knew him, these were the preliminaries to what his colleagues always referred to as his sessions with himself. It was not unknown at the end of the session for the piece of paper still to be virgin white and the pencil untouched, but that in no way indicated that the exercise had been a failure. In fact, there was seldom ever anything more than a few disconnected words and some genuinely ornamental doodling.

Manton gazed at the sheet of paper and slowly picked up the pencil. There seemed to be one obvious starting point for his thoughts, namely the three deaths, P.C. Moss, Tarrant and Pinty. The last two were obviously connected in some way. Was the first also? Putting that on one side for the moment, it was now quite clear to Manton that Pinty had shot Tarrant; that seemed to be beyond all dispute. Then Pinty had either committed suicide or been murdered. The simpler and tidier theory was obviously the former, and furthermore it was possible to see why he had killed himself; namely to avoid the hangman's rope. But supposing Pinty had not been the cause of his own death; supposing in fact that he had been murdered. By whom, and why, and exactly when? The only possible reason could be revenge for his having murdered Tarrant. There must be some sort of feud about it. Maybe Tarrant was a member of a gang and when one of his friends saw Pinty shoot him down as he was about to enter the witness box, that became Pinty's own death warrant. And of course, if there was a feud angle, that would presumably mean that Tarrant's friends would know of Pinty's existence and even know Pinty. From the fact that Pinty had committed a daring and cold-blooded murder, it was clear that he was not the ordinary peaceful little suburban dweller that he'd always passed himself off to be. And then again, on that theory, the 'when' element was more easily accounted for. The post-mortem examination revealed that Pinty had been dead about forty-eight hours; that would mean that he could have been shot pretty soon after he disappeared from the Old Bailey. Obviously he'd been followed from there and in some way lured to his death.

Manton sat back and surveyed his train of thought. It was logical if a trifle improbable. But then so many unlikely things had already happened in this case that improbability in itself was not a defect in the hypothesis.

It seemed to him that at the moment, suicide and murder were running neck and neck and he fervently wished that something would come to light which would knock one or other of them out. The fact that Dr. Craig didn't think suicide probable was almost the only fly in that pot of ointment; in every other respect it was the neater and more logical solution. Suddenly he revolted against his theory of Mr. Pinty having become involved in some form of underworld activity. It was just too fantastic. But then again the man had committed a murder in full view of a hundred people, and wasn't that equally fantastic?

Idly he opened the drawer of his desk and pulled out the Pinty dossier. As he did so, a photograph fell from it on to the floor. He leant over the side of his chair and picked it up and put it on top of the file which lay on the desk before him. He slowly nodded his head at the photo and spoke as he did so.

'You're an unexpected one, aren't you?' and, after a pause: 'If only you could tell me why you shot Tarrant, I might be able to decide why somebody found it necessary to kill you or why you had to kill yourself. You look such a law-abiding little fellow too. I wonder . . .' Suddenly he stopped and stared intently at the unsmiling and solemn countenance of Mr. Pinty. It was a comparatively recent photograph which Mrs. Pinty had given them at their request when they first visited her. It was a photo which had subsequently appeared in all the national press when the great hunt for the little man was on.

With an exclamation, Manton bounded from his chair and out of the room. A few paces down the corridor brought him to the office which Sergeant Talper shared with two other Detective Sergeants. The former, who knew that Manton was having one of his sessions with himself, was taking the opportunity of catching up with some of the more routine and clerical aspects of solving a murder.

He looked up as Manton exploded into the room holding Mr. Pinty's photograph in his right hand and thrust it under his gaze.

'Look at that photo, Andy!'

'Yes, it's Pinty; the one his wife gave us', said Sergeant Talper not quite knowing what sort of comment was expected of him.

'Of course it's Pinty, but is that exactly how he looked when he sat on the jury that day?'

Sergeant Talper thought a moment before answering.

'As far as I know, yes. What are you getting at, sir?'

'Don't you see, that in this photo he's wearing a pair of gold-rimmed spectacles with thick lenses, and didn't his wife tell us that he always wore them?'

'Yes, I remember she did, because you asked her when she handed it to us if that was exactly as he always appeared, and she said "yes", and added that he was useless without his spectacles.'

Manton looked triumphant when he spoke.

'Well he managed to commit suicide without them; or lose them in the course of getting murdered. There were no spectacles anywhere around him on Hampstead Heath.' He paused before concluding thoughtfully: 'Now I wonder just what is the significance of that?'

Chapter Seventeen

TALPER accompanied Manton back to his room where the latter gave him a resumé of the various theories with which he had been toying.

'I don't yet know, Andy, what the significance of the spectacles is, but I feel it in my bones that something important is going to turn upon their disappearance. For a start, it weakens, if it doesn't actually knock out, the suicide theory, because it's hardly conceivable that Pinty, who we know couldn't see a cow in a field without them, would throw them away before killing himself. There's no rhyme or reason why he should, and apart from that, he could never have got to where we found him without them.'

Sergeant Talper nodded his agreement.

'Of course if it was murder, sir, the murderer would have every reason to deprive Pinty of his spectacles. By doing that he went a long way to incapacitating him.'

'You're right, Andy. It wouldn't be very difficult for the murderer to get them off, and with the unfortunate Pinty then floundering about, he could shoot him at very close range without the latter ever knowing what was about to happen to him.'

Exactly how significant a clue Manton now had in his hands, he was not to realize fully till considerably later when other startling events had happened, and in such swift succession that he began to feel that it was like some nightmare promotion test where every conceivable eventuality takes place and one is never given time to recover from one situation before being overwhelmed by the next.

It was Sergeant Talper who spoke next.

'It looks, sir, as though your feud theory is the right one and Pinty was killed to avenge the murder of Tarrant.'

At that moment there was a knock on the door and a young Detective Constable, who looked no older than a sixth form school boy, burst in. He had a message form in his hand and he handed it excitedly to Manton.

'This has just come in, sir.' Manton took the form and the young C.I.D. man went on excitedly: 'It looks a pretty hot piece of news, sir.'

'Thanks, Farley. You may be right at that', said Manton. 'Listen to this, Andy. This is a message to say that two people by the names of Jakes Hartman and Maisie Jenks got married by special licence at a Register Office this morning.' He looked up at Sergeant Talper whose face registered a proper degree of incredulous surprise and went on: 'I think that we'll sally forth and visit father Jenks to see what he's got to say about this. If he doesn't know it already, it'll be interesting to observe his reaction when we tell him about his new son-in-law.'

The two officers gathered their hats and coats and went downstairs to where Manton's car was waiting. The driver had to be extracted from the canteen, but soon they were on their way and about twenty minutes later were standing on the doorstep of the Jenks home in St. John's Wood.

Manton rang the bell. There was no answer and he rang it again longer and looked up at the windows at the front of the house.

'They're not shut and locked, so presumably there's somebody at home.'

Almost as he spoke, the door silently opened and there staring out at them with no visible expression of welcome on her features was an ageing female.

'Good afternoon—is Mr. Jenks at home?'

'Can't 'ear yer.'

Manton remembered having previously heard something about a deaf servant, so produced one of his cards and in a voice which proclaimed his presence to the whole postal district, he bellowed at the old woman.

'I'm Chief Inspector Manton from New Scotland Yard. I want to see Mr. Jenks. Is he in?'

At this, she unceremoniously beckoned them in with her head and closed the door behind them. Leading the way, she took them along the hall and without a word showed them into a room which looked on to the garden at the back. The door closed and the two men found themselves alone. It seemed to Manton that they waited an age in a house which was as silent as the grave and he was beginning to wonder if anyone was at home at all when suddenly the door opened and in walked Maisie Jenks' father.

Manton immediately noticed that he looked tired and worried, and that he gave the impression of not having had very much sleep recently.

He nodded to both the officers.

'Good afternoon, Inspector. I'm sorry to have kept you waiting but the fact is I was having forty winks on my bed when old Harriet told me you were here.'

'I'm sorry we've disturbed you, Mr. Jenks, but there are one or two things I want to have a word with you

113

about, and the best way seemed to come out and pay you a call.'

The other motioned them to be seated and then sat down himself at the far side of his desk so that their impression of being granted an interview was heightened.

Jenks remained silent and obviously intended that the police officers should open the conversation by stating their business.

After a moment's pause, Manton, placing the tips of his fingers together and then contemplating the effect, spoke.

'Well first, Mr. Jenks, have you had any news of your daughter?'

'Not a word. I was hoping you would be able to tell me something on that score', replied Jenks. 'As you can probably realize, Inspector, I'm desperately worried about her sudden disappearance and I've hardly slept a wink since she went.'

Manton waited a moment but when the other didn't go on, he said: 'We had news of your daughter shortly before we left the Yard, and I thought you might have heard it too.'

'I tell you I've heard nothing. What information have you got?' Jenks' voice was tense and taut as he spoke.

Manton watched him very carefully and then slowly said: 'Our information is that your daughter got married at a Register Office this morning.'

'Got married?' Jenks sounded genuinely incredulous. 'Got married? To whom?'

'Apparently she married a man called Jakes Hartman', replied Manton still watching him intently.

It was manifest that Jenks was maintaining a very tight control of his nerves and was determined to display the minimum of emotion. When he spoke again, it was in a quiet and almost off-hand tone.

'Wasn't he the shorthand writer at the trial? I know Maisie knew him but she certainly never said anything to me about marrying him.'

'Her marriage seems to have been as sudden as her departure from home', said Manton dryly and then suddenly switched the subject. 'Who lives in this house, Mr. Jenks, besides yourself?'

Jenks looked momentarily surprised.

'My son, Ronald—you've never met him and he's out at the moment. Maisie did until she left, and old Harriet; that's all.' And as if in answer to Manton's unasked question, he added: 'I'm a widower.'

Nobody spoke for a minute or two. Manton was satisfied that the news of his daughter's marriage had come as a considerable shock to Jenks and that he had had no foreknowledge of the event.

Jenks got up from his chair and walked round to the fireplace where he suddenly spoke with his back turned on the officers. 'Why do you think, Inspector, that my daughter should have acted in this way?'

He remained facing the wall and Manton regarded his rear view for a while before answering.

'So far as we know, your daughter was the one person in Court who saw something vital in the commission of the murder. That's the only possible explanation of her scream just prior to the firing of the shot. If it was the juror, Pinty, who murdered Tarrant, was there any reason for her to have acted as she has; that is, to have run away from home without a word to anyone and to have got married? Personally I don't see it. But of course if she saw someone she knew about to fire the fatal shot, that would be sufficient reason for her to scream and do a genuine faint. Suppose that person was able to persuade her to run away with him and marry him, that would effectively seal the lips of the only witness against him, because a wife can't be made to give evidence against her husband in a case such as this; she's not a competent witness for the crown in such circumstances.'

Sergeant Talper had been watching Manton intently as he propounded this fresh theory founded in the light of new circumstances. When he had finished speaking, Jenks turned round.

'So you think I've got a murderer for a son-in-law?'

And he gave Manton a queer little smile as he spoke.

Chapter Eighteen

AFTER they had left the house and were driving back to the Yard, Sergeant Talper turned to Manton.

'Do you really think Hartman is a suspect now, sir, or was that just something you put over for the benefit of our friend Jenks?'

At first Talper didn't think that Manton had heard him, since he continued to gaze out of the window at the cold and hurrying figures on the pavement who melted in and out of the thickening fog. And when he did start speaking, he continued to stare out at the gloomy prospect.

'Perhaps a bit of both, Andy. It's certainly the only logical explanation of their getting married in that sudden and secret fashion. And it's a piece of devilish cunning into the bargain.'

He paused and Talper broke in: 'But if it was Hartman who shot Tarrant—apart from the fact that he had no motive so far as we know—why then did Pinty have to do a vanishing trick and shoot himself dead?'

'I know, Andy. Never was there a case in which motive was so vital, and we're as near to pinning a motive on to anyone as to putting the late Commissioner's ghost in a strait-jacket. However, as you and I know, we don't have to prove a motive. If we get enough evidence to charge somebody with murder, we needn't bother our heads with the motives which are so beloved of the story-writers.'

'And juries', said Talper. 'It doesn't matter how many times you tell a jury that the motive doesn't matter and the Crown don't have to prove one, the fact remains that they like to be given one. It helps them make up their uneasy minds.' He spoke with conviction as he went on: 'You know that, sir, as well as I do. Unless you do prove a motive, a jury is apt to think that you've got hold of the wrong person however strong the rest of your evidence may be.'

Manton turned and smiled.

'Yes, you're absolutely right. And I agree that until we find some sort of a motive here, we shall go on floundering around. Certain bits of the puzzle seem to fit and then just as you're thinking along one particular line, you find other bits which also fit together but which completely fail to match the first.' Talper could see that Manton was thinking hard as he spoke, and he didn't interrupt. 'The one thing we've been taking for granted is that Pinty murdered Tarrant,' went on Manton, 'but I'm not so sure now that that's an assumption which ought to exclude all others. Pinty was not the only one with opportunity. Glindy, MacBruce and Hartman, were all just as close to Tarrant when he met his death. All had equal opportunity, as, for that matter, did that exotic woman in green, Miss Fenwick-Blunt. Remember, Andy, that from the time Pinty dashed out of the Court to the time when we found his body up on Hampstead Heath, only one man ever saw him and spoke to him so far as we know.'

Sergeant Talper looked surprised for a moment.

'You mean the Judge's usher in the corridor outside the Court.'

'Exactly,' said Manton, 'and you'll recall that according to him Pinty dashed past him and said something to the effect that he'd seen the person with the gun and that it had been pointed at him too.' Manton waited to make sure that Talper was following him before going on: 'If that's true, doesn't it mean this? That Pinty saw who shot Tarrant, and the murderer knew that Pinty saw. That explains why the gun was pointed at Pinty and the poor frightened little man just took to his heels and ran. The murderer knew that so long as Pinty lived, his life was in his, Pinty's, hands, and the only way to stop Pinty from talking was to shut his mouth for ever.' He paused and concluded: 'And that's precisely what has happened. Pinty has been brutally and effectively silenced.'

As he finished speaking, the car nosed its way off the Embankment and turned into Scotland Yard, and the two officers got out.

Manton went straight up to his room and Talper went along to see whether anything new had come in while they had been out. He joined the former in a few minutes.

'Nothing', he said laconically.

'It's high time Mr. and Mrs. Jakes Hartman were unearthed and dished up', said Manton. 'Obviously they haven't hung around the area where they got married. But with all the press hue and cry after them they can't have got very far. Frankly I'm surprised they've been able to remain unspotted for as long as this. The more I think of it, the more I'm certain that Maisie Jenks' scream is the starting point of this case and the clue to both the murders.' He walked over to the window and gazed out at the uninviting view. Then he turned about. 'This might be a suitable moment to make our little inquiry about Inspector MacBruce. There's something odd about that man and he's not acting normally for someone in his position. And it isn't just his North of the Border manner either.' As he spoke, he walked over to the door. 'I think I'll go and get permission from the Assistant Commissioner to have a squint at his personal file. It might produce something of interest.'

He left the room and Talper waited. It was about twenty minutes later when Manton returned with a file beneath his arm. He sat down at his desk and placed it before him.

'You'd better bring up a chair, Andy, so that you can look at it as well.'

Details of the Scottish Inspector's antecedent service were contained in the large and somewhat tattered sheaf of papers before them. The date of his birth, his schooling, dates of joining the force and a complete list of his moves and transfers as well as a list of commendations were all recorded.

'Doesn't look as though there's much here', said Manton turning the dog-eared pages. 'Wonder if he's been in any bother since he's been in the Force. Most of us kick over the official traces at times, but it's all a question of how you do it and whether you get caught.' Suddenly he sat up straight in his chair. 'This looks more interesting.' He read aloud from the back of a document which he held up in his left hand. 'Reprimanded and loss of seniority for ill-treating a man in custody but not then charged. That was in 1937 when he was stationed at North West London Police Station, and the man whom he knocked about was named

William Edgar Tarrant!' Manton put the document back on top of the file. 'Now I wonder, Andy, who could give us some more details of the story behind that entry?'

He lifted the receiver of his phone and asked for a number. After a pause, he spoke.

'Hello—is that North West London? Detective Chief Inspector Manton of C. one here. Wonder if you can tell me who was your Station Sergeant in July nineteen thirty-seven. . . . Yes, that's right, thirty-seven.'

He was silent for a moment while someone the other end went to ferret out the required information.

'Hello—yes. Oh, Sergeant MacBruce, was it? Can you now tell me who was in charge of the Station at that time?' There was more silence while he waited and then: 'Inspector Penny, was it? Any idea where I can find him now? Probably dead', he said in an aside to Talper. 'Hello—yes, still here—oh fine, thanks a lot', and he wrote an address on the blotter before him as he replaced the receiver in its cradle.

He smiled a pleased and happy smile at Sergeant Talper.

'Inspector Penny is not dead after all. He's only retired and living down at Kingston where I gather he can be found amongst his tomatoes and chrysanthemums: though I should have hardly thought so at this time of year.'

Manton closed the MacBruce file, unlocked a drawer in his desk, put it in and relocked it. 'I think a trip to Kingston straight away is called for; even though it is a beastly evening.'

Once more the two men put on hats and coats and left the building, so famous throughout the world and

121

without whose existence many excellent books would never have been written and many bad films never been made—and vice versa.

It was a long and tedious journey out to Kingston. The fog was extremely bad in patches and everywhere it was chill and dank. They had considerable difficulty in finding Inspector Penny's house, it being just a number in a neat, suburban road of quite attractive little homes, all looking exactly alike. Finally Sergeant Talper had to get out and walk along the pavement feeling the numbers on each gate and reading them like braille. When Number forty-four was found Manton got out and the two officers went up the short concrete path which led to the front door. There was a further pause as they groped for a bell. Shortly after, a light came on in the hall and the front door opened.

A homely middle-aged woman stood on the threshold peering out.

'Mrs. Penny?' asked Manton.

'Yes, what can I do for you?'

'I'm Detective Chief Inspector Manton of Scotland Yard and this is Sergeant Talper. Is your husband in, Mrs. Penny? We'd rather like to see him on a matter of some importance.'

'You'd better come in', said Mrs. Penny and at the same time she turned and shouted down the hall: 'Alfred, there are two gentlemen from Scotland Yard here to see you.'

The door at the end of the hall, which obviously led into the kitchen, opened and through it came a large burly individual. He had a pleasant red face and crinkly iron-grey hair and he was dressed just right for supper in the kitchen on a winter's evening.

Once more Manton introduced himself and apologized for calling unexpectedly and at such an inconvenient hour, as it was clear that the Pennys were in the middle of their evening meal.

Ex-Inspector Penny brushed aside Manton's apologies with a friendly smile and invited them along to the cosy room from which he had emerged.

'I've never had the pleasure of meeting you, Inspector Manton, but of course I know your name. The newspapers see to that.' He grinned and went on: 'You've got your hands pretty full at the moment, haven't you?'

Manton returned the grin.

'I certainly have and it's just about the most baffling case I've had charge of. It's to do with one aspect of it that we've come to see you on this filthy evening.'

The ex-policeman nodded.

'I thought as much and I think I can probably go further and guess exactly which aspect it is that's brought you here.' He paused and then said: 'Mac-Bruce?'

'You're right again', said Manton.

By this time Mrs. Penny who had been working in the background placed before the visitors two large and steaming cups of tea. It was her husband who spoke. 'I'm afraid it's the best hospitality we can offer you in the circumstances.'

Manton and Talper signified their appreciation, and as the former slowly stirred his tea, he started speaking again.

'As you obviously know, MacBruce was the Court Inspector in Number One Court at the Old Bailey on the day when Tarrant was so dramatically murdered.

123

In fact, he was within touching distance of him when the shot was fired. Since then he has acted . . . well, shall I say he hasn't been as frank as one would expect a brother officer to be. It so happened that I was to-day looking through his personal file and saw that he'd been in a bit of trouble in thirty-seven for knocking some suspect about. I needn't add that I was more than interested when I also saw who that suspect was!' Here there was a pause, while Manton picked up his cup and sipped his tea. Inspector Penny, who had been watching him all the time he spoke, still kept his gaze upon him. Manton went on: 'Well it wasn't a very far step from learning that to our arrival here. What I really want to know, Mr. Penny, is what actually led up to that affair and more especially what the association between Tarrant and MacBruce was fifteen years ago.'

'In the first place,' said Inspector Penny, 'I realize your inquiry is an official one made in the course of duty but, so far as you can, I'd like you to regard what I tell you as being off the record. I haven't seen MacBruce since I retired in thirty-nine. He was never a particular friend of mine, but he's still in the force and I shouldn't like any opinion I might give of him to be used officially. It wouldn't be right to prejudice him in that way.' He paused and gave Manton a querying look.

The latter nodded understandingly. 'That couldn't be fairer and shall certainly be the basis of our talk.'

But before Manton finished Inspector Penny had started talking again, taking the assurance for granted.

'MacBruce was Station Sergeant at North West London when I was in charge there. He was an efficient and unpopular officer. I don't think anyone really liked him, either his colleagues or the less fortunate citizens who came into official contact with him. Tarrant was well known in the district and though he was a crook, he was quite a likeable one. On this particular occasion he was brought in on some false-pretence charge. The details don't matter. As usual he was pretty cocky and I suppose he got under Sergeant MacBruce's skin. Anyway the next thing is that the latter has charged him on rather flimsy evidence and Tarrant is nursing a very black eye and a fine swollen lip. He demanded to see the Divisional Surgeon and in due course that worthy entered his findings in the Station log book. I told MacBruce that he was all kinds of a fool and might well find himself later in a very sticky position. And thats'. exactly how it turned out. Tarrant kept quite quiet about it all till he came up at Quarter Sessions. Then the defence subpœnaed the Divisional Surgeon, called evidence to show that when he was arrested his eyes weren't black and his lips weren't swollen, and before you knew where you were, the jury had acquitted him and the Chairman had said some pretty outspoken things about MacBruce. Well, you know what happened in the end, but as near as dammit he was chucked out.' The ex-policeman shook his head in memory of it all and went on: 'MacBruce took his coating extremely badly. He didn't seem to think he was darned lucky to have his job still, and he wouldn't listen to anyone who told him he was.'

Here Inspector Penny paused again and looking straight at Manton said with great seriousness: 'Now I don't think MacBruce is a murderer from what I knew of him, but I've told you the full facts of the incident as I remember them and the truth is that afterwards he went about swearing all sorts of vengeance against

Tarrant whom he regarded as being entirely responsible for his misfortune. Though he never said any such thing in my presence, I know he did even hint at murder to some of the other officers—in implied terms of course; I don't mean he uttered direct threats.'

A silence followed this recital of the events of fifteen years ago and Manton was the first to break it.

'I'm very grateful to you, Mr. Penny, for giving us such a full account. As you say, MacBruce doesn't seem like a murderer; but then probably the same thing was said of Crippen and Smith and Armstrong in their time. The fact remains that fifteen years ago he uttered murderous threats of a sort against a man who three days ago was killed by a murderer's bullet; and at the time of the murder MacBruce was as close to the victim as Talper is to me; and what is more, he could have fired the fatal shot.'

This brief but epitomized exposition of the case against MacBruce was followed by a profound silence.

Chapter Nineteen

MANTON and Talper stayed on at Inspector Penny's house quite a time after the official side of their visit had been accomplished. It's the same all the world over when members of the same profession get together. Personalities are discussed, the younger ones ask their older comrades about their experiences of yesteryear, and the latter listen with interest and occasional scorn to stories of the new ways. So it was in the Pennys' kitchen on this foggy November evening, with Mrs. Penny keeping the company well supplied with cups of tea.

At last the time came when Manton got up and said they really must leave. The fog outside had lifted slightly and the two Yard men swirled away from the kerb in their car as ex-Inspector Penny gave them a final wave before closing the front door.

For some time, they drove in silence, and then Manton turned to his companion and said suddenly: 'I think, Andy, we'll pay a call on Miss Fenwick-Blunt on our way back. I'd like it to be a surprise visit and we'll catch her in her own lair. There are one or two things I'd like to ask her about and her answers should be all the better for not being prepared.'

He gave the necessary instructions to the driver and it was about half-past nine when the car pulled up outside the undistinguished-looking hotel where Miss Fenwick-Blunt lived. Manton, followed by Talper, got out and strode across the ill-lit pavement and up two steps to the front door of the place. It was open and the

127

two officers walked into the small hall. On the right were two uncomfortable looking armchairs and a brown leather sofa whose bulging springs gave it a contour line somewhat like a relief map of the Pyrenees. On the left was a small desk with the usual sort of articles standing on it.

The whole place seemed to be deserted, when from upstairs there suddenly came the sounds of running feet and voices, and a prematurely aged female wearing pince-nez and a black-satin dress with a well-worn black cardigan over it swept down the stairs at a speed quite unnatural to her sombre appearance. She was followed by a harassed looking maid whose straggling ends of hair fell out around her cap.

The black-satin female was clearly in two minds about whether to recognize the presence of the two officers or to ignore them completely. At the bottom of the stairs she wavered for a moment before scuttling away down the passage which led through gloom and a smell of yesterday's kippers to the back of the house. Before she had time to make up her mind, Manton stepped forward and spoke.

'Could you kindly tell me where I can find Miss Fenwick-Blunt?'

Sergeant Talper at first thought that the woman's eyes were going to pop right out of her head. As it was her pince-nez wiggled dangerously and she shot her right hand up to steady them.

When she spoke the words came out like a series of small nervous explosions.

'Who are you and why do you want to see Miss Fenwick-Blunt? Anyway you can't see her because something's happened.'

'Madam, I don't know what you mean by something's happened but we're from Scotland Yard and you'd better tell me exactly what it is.'

The woman's eyes still looked in danger of falling out and it was with something of a gasp that she repeated the words: from Scotland Yard. Then speaking with obvious relief, she said: 'Thank goodness you're here! I was just about to go out and fetch a policeman—or rather Ada was'—here she signified the harassed housemaid who was still hovering just behind her on the penultimate step. 'Something dreadful has just happened. Someone's tried to murder poor Miss Fenwick-Blunt.'

She paused dramatically and it was the turn of Manton's eyes to behave abnormally.

'Murder her!' he repeated.

'Yes,' she went on, 'he hid in her room and when she went up after coffee this evening, he sprang out at her with a revolver.'

'Did he hit her?' asked Manton.

'Oh, no, he didn't touch her.'

'I mean with the revolver.'

'Oh, no, he didn't fire it because she screamed and he jumped out of the window.' As if this might have sounded a bit too much like Don Juan, she added, 'There's a fire escape just outside Miss Fenwick-Blunt's window and he must have climbed down that way.'

'How long ago did this happen?'

'Oh, inside the hour; definitely inside the hour. I was sitting in one of those easy chairs.' Here she pointed at one of the two Manton had already noticed, 'when I heard the scream. I was talking to Mrs. Chatterbrick at the time and I said to her "Good heavens, Mrs. Chatterbrick, who on earth's that screaming?" No sooner had I said it than Miss Fenwick-Blunt came out of her room on to the landing and screamed again.' She paused for breath before resuming what had become a veritable torrent of words. 'I immediately dashed up and by that time Miss Blunt had gone back into her room and was sitting on the edge of her bed— proper white she was. "What on earth's happened, Miss Blunt?" I said: "you look as though you've seen a ghost." "A dreadful man wearing a mask tried to kill me", she gasped. "I'm so nervous, don't leave me, Miss Laxton," she went on—so then I called to Ada and when she came up . . .'

Manton could see that there might be no end to this tale if he let it take its course, so somewhat brusquely he interrupted the flow.

'I think, Miss Laxton, my colleague and I had best go up and see Miss Blunt straight away if you'll show us the way.'

Well, if the police aren't interested in the evidence, that's their look out, thought Miss Laxton. Aloud she said, 'I'll go ahead and tell her that you're here, so that she can receive you properly.' She sounded absurdly coy when she said this and hurriedly went on: 'Normally of course our lady guests don't have men up to their bedrooms at all—unless of course, it's someone like the doctor.'

She turned and remounted the stairs followed by Ada and the two officers. When they got to the second floor, she tapped on a door and without waiting for an answer disappeared inside the room, shutting the door behind her. Manton and Talper were left on the landing with

Ada, who continued to stare at them as if they were specimens in a tank. Suddenly without warning she spoke.

'Pity someone don't bump off a few of the old cows properly.' Her voice was curiously matter-of-fact and having delivered herself of this considered view, she shrugged her shoulders and went up to the next floor.

The door of Miss Fenwick-Blunt's bedroom opened and Miss Laxton beckoned to the two men, with a long bony finger. As they entered, she whispered: 'I'll go and ring the doctor. She'll need a sleeping draught after all this.'

Although stripped of her forest green plumage, Miss Fenwick-Blunt still looked like some rather ridiculous but exotic bird. She was sitting in bed propped up by two large pillows. Round her shoulders was a faded pink quilted bed jacket, and round her neck was the gold chain of the inimitable lorgnette. As the officers entered she emitted a deep sigh and turned her head to give them a wan greeting. She sighed again before speaking.

'I've had a terrible experience, Inspector. I could see murder in his eyes. I was sure he was going to kill me.'

'Perhaps you'd better start at the beginning', said Manton quietly.

'Well, after we'd finished coffee this evening, I remembered that I'd left my library book up in my room so I came up to get it.' She paused to look at the two officers in turn to make sure that each was giving his fullest attention to the dramatic narrative on which she had embarked. 'I turned on the light as I entered my room and came over to the bedside table where

131

my book was, when I suddenly heard a vague rustling sound behind me. I just casually glanced over my shoulder and there was this murderer.' Here there was a longer and more dramatic pause, and Miss Fenwick-Blunt added a shudder to her repertoire of sighs before going on. 'He had a revolver in his right hand and it was pointing straight at me. The lower half of his face was covered by a white scarf and he was wearing a hat well pulled down over his eyes so that I could really see very little of his face. I think he had on a mackintosh, but I really can't remember for certain.' This time the pause became so long that Manton felt constrained to urge her on.

'What happened then?' he said.

'He muttered something about the murder the other day and told me I'd better keep my mouth shut or I'd be a corpse as well.'

The Inspector gazed intently at her as she reached this part of her story.

'Did you know exactly what he was referring to?' he asked.

'I naturally thought he meant the murder of that poor man Tarrant.' Miss Blunt didn't wait for any further interruptions but sailed on: 'Then I screamed as loud as I could and the man opened the window and jumped out on to the fire escape. And while he was doing that, I went on to the landing and screamed again. Miss Laxton closed the window after she came up', she concluded as she noticed Manton looking at it.

He moved over to it and peered closely and then gingerly he opened it and looked out. An iron fire escape which came down the side of the house from

the roof passed just to the left of it and provided
a simple method of entry or exit. He looked intently
at the window ledge before turning to Sergeant
Talper.

'There don't appear to be any fresh marks, but you'd
better go down and see what happens at the bottom. It
appears to finish in a yard and I'd like to know how one
gets in and out of it.'

Sergeant Talper leant out beside Manton and then
left the room, leaving him alone with Miss Fenwick-
Blunt.

Manton looked into the corner beside the heavy
wardrobe where the intruder must obviously have been
hiding when Miss Blunt came into the room. While he
did so, she lay back against her wedge of pillows with
eyes closed. He cast her several covert glances and
wished he had the attributes of a mind reader. He
cleared his throat and she opened her eyes after a suitable pause.

'Well, Inspector?'

Manton met her gaze and held it, before replying
with equal deliberation.

'Have you any idea at all as to who this intruder was?
I know you say that he had most of his face covered up,
but if you think hard you may remember something
familiar about his voice or the expression in his eyes
which would give us a lead.'

Miss Fenwick-Blunt appeared to think hard before
replying.

'What little I could see of his face looked white and
it might have been rather a pointed one. I shouldn't
have said he was either young or old—you know, somewhere in his late thirties.'

Here she paused and looked at Manton as if to try and gauge his reaction to her description.

'Anything about his voice?'

'No, I certainly didn't recognize his voice.'

'Just tell me again exactly what it was that he said.'

Miss Fenwick-Blunt shuddered before replying.

'It was something like "if you don't keep your mouth shut, you'll become a corpse as well".'

It was clear that she didn't at all relish the word 'corpse' in reference to herself and Manton couldn't help being secretly amused at the intruder's lack of descriptive taste.

'Has anything else happened since the murder of Tarrant to make you think that someone was trying to threaten you?' he asked.

Miss Blunt looked almost shamefaced before replying. 'Well there was the note.'

'What note?'

'Well, I'm afraid I've been a bit silly about that. You see, I didn't take it seriously and I destroyed it without telling anyone about it.'

'You'd better tell me about it now. When did you get it, where did it come from, and what did it say?'

'I got it yesterday morning at breakfast time. It was on my table with other letters when I came down. It was a cheap envelope with a tuppenny halfpenny stamp on it, and the name and address were printed in capitals. I think it was postmarked somewhere down in south-east London. Yes, it was Brixton, I remember now.' Manton stood motionless watching her closely as she recounted her story. 'Inside the envelope was a cheap, plain piece of paper and on it was drawn a picture of a man hanging from a gallows and beneath it was printed, BEWARE OR YOU TOO.'

'Why did you destroy it?'

Miss Blunt didn't appear to be put out either by the question or the severity of Manton's tone.

'Well, Inspector, I'm a woman of the world, and I just didn't take it seriously. I thought it was the work of some crank or feeble-minded creature who'd seen my name mentioned in one of the papers and decided to indulge his crankiness or madness by sending me this note.'

'Did you just tear it up and leave it on the table or...'

Before Manton could finish his question, the reply came shortly and firmly: 'No, I burnt it.'

'I still can't understand how you failed to notify the police about this, Miss Blunt, especially after what had just happened. It was most reprehensible of you.'

Manton was distinctly annoyed with this tiresome woman who first of all told him interminable stories which hardly helped him at all and called on him late at night to unburden herself of them, and then when something important like this note happened, she destroyed it and said not a word to anyone. It really was too exasperating for words. However there it was for the moment and he couldn't think of anything further to be done at the hotel.

He was about to leave the room when he accidentally knocked a book off the small bedside table. He stooped to pick it up and saw that a small piece of paper had fallen out on to the floor. This he retrieved and was about to put back into the book when he happened to see what was written on it. Miss Fenwick-Blunt had been unable to see what had happened and so Manton's expression of surprise also eluded her. He replaced the book on the table but the small piece of paper was no longer between the leaves. It lay instead in his pocket and on it was written the name and address of Prison Officer Albert Glindy.

Chapter Twenty

As the two men drove away from Kensington, Manton turned to Talper and said:

'Find anything of interest down in the yard, Andy?'

'No, nothing. That fire escape finishes up near the kitchen window. There's a door which leads from the yard to the front of the premises, but it wasn't locked so it was quite easy for the intruder to walk out and nobody need have seen him at all.' Sergeant Talper paused and went on: 'I gather that the cook was the only person in the kitchen at the time.'

'Is that our friend Ada?'

'No, Ada's the sort of housemaid and she was somewhere upstairs, probably with a head full of murderous ideas to judge from her only remark to us. The cook's name is Ethel and she struck me as being an absolute slut of a woman. If her cooking is in keeping with her appearance, it's surprising they haven't all been done in a long time ago.' Ethel seemed to have made a considerable impression on Sergeant Talper for he went on: 'If my old mother had seen a kitchen like that Ethel's, she'd have boxed her ears and given both of them a darn good scrubbing. Anyway Ethel neither saw nor heard anything. I tried a little experiment with her. Having told her to stand in the kitchen and stir one of her filthy saucepans, I mounted the fire escape and then came down from the height of the first floor and went through the yard and out by the door.'

'And did she hear you?' asked Manton.

'She did not, because she thought I wanted her to stop up her ears. But in any event it seemed to me to be perfectly possible to get away quietly without anyone in the kitchen necessarily hearing anything.'

'No signs on the ground or anything of that sort?'

'No. I climbed the escape right up as far as Miss Blunt's bedroom and could find no scratches, bits of torn clothing or anything significant at all.'

Manton shook his head and combed his lower lip with his top teeth.

'This case is just about as baffling as it could be. I almost wonder if that old girl hasn't made up the whole thing for some reason of her own. If she has, I'll darn well see her prosecuted for public mischief', he added vehemently.

Sergeant Talper looked surprised.

'You don't seriously think she's invented it, do you?'

'I suppose not, but only because I can't think of any earthly reason why she should. Or is there a reason?' he said thoughtfully. After a pause he went on: 'It's like this, Andy. The Fenwick-Blunt woman is one of five who had the opportunity of murdering Tarrant. Supposing in fact she did do it, mightn't she well now devise this little drama to throw us off the scent. You see, she told us in the first place that she didn't know who fired the shot as she was distracted by Maisie Jenks' scream at the crucial moment. Later she delicately suggested that it might have been Glindy who dropped the revolver afterwards. Well, this little affair staged to-night—assuming that it was a put-up job—was designed to show that someone, who was obviously the murderer of Tarrant, was threatening her life if she disclosed what she knew about the murder. According to her she's told us all she knows and it isn't very much.'

Talper broke in at this point.

'But surely it's quite possible for the murderer to think that she must have seen something vital, something which if disclosed would mean his immediate arrest.'

'I haven't yet told you of two other interesting matters', said Manton. He then briefly recounted what Miss Fenwick-Blunt had told him of the threatening note she had received. 'And just before I was leaving, this bit of paper fell out of a book which I accidentally knocked off her bedside table.'

Manton fished the piece of paper from his pocket and passed it to Sergeant Talper as he spoke. Talper studied it carefully and then slowly passed it back.

'What do you make of it, sir?'

'What do I make of it?' echoed Manton. 'It persuades me even more that she concocted the whole of this evening's entertainment for our benefit, and an extremely cunning performance it was. In the first place, she's too clever to identify the mysterious intruder, but such few details as she does give us, fit, amongst others, our friend Glindy. And then in describing the envelope in which the threatening note came, she added almost as an afterthought that she seemed to recall that it bore the Brixton postmark. She, of course, knows that Glindy is a warder at Brixton Prison and furthermore she knows his address and has gone to the trouble of writing it down on a piece of paper for some reason or another. For what reason, I wonder? You see, the whole thing could have been subtly designed to lead us to Glindy. But why should she want to do that? Surely the only answer is that she wished to distract our attention from herself, since it was she who in fact murdered Tarrant. Come to think of it, she's just the sort of old girl that Tarrant used to get hold of and enmesh in that extraordinary way of his.'

It was manifest that Sergeant Talper didn't like Manton's new theory and he shook his head.

'It doesn't make proper sense, sir. And you haven't explained the bit of paper you've got in your pocket. Why should she have Glindy's name and address? Also it wasn't as if she played that into your hands. From what you say she doesn't even know you've got it. That was hardly planted for your benefit.'

Manton thought for a while before answering.

'It's possible that if I hadn't knocked over the book myself, she'd have done so, knowing that I would pick it up and see the bit of paper.'

'But with what object?' asked Talper relentlessly. 'If your theory is correct, and she was by infinitely subtle and cunning means putting you on to Glindy's scent, why the bit of paper with his name and address on it? There's none of the earlier finesse about that.' He could see that Manton was listening attentively to what he said. 'Frankly, sir, I don't pretend to be able to offer you the explanation of that bit of paper but it does strike me as being completely out of tune with your theory.'

'Well, Andy, what is your view then?' asked Manton.

'At the moment, I see no reason to doubt that someone did get into her bedroom and do just what she said he did and then depart the way he came. Since we ourselves find it difficult to believe that she didn't see anything of the murderer, isn't it more than likely that person thinks the same thing?'

'In fact,' said Manton, 'you think she told us a genuine story and that the fact that what she said points to Glindy having been her uninvited visitor, and therefore by inference Tarrant's murderer, is something which we ought to follow up.' The Sergeant nodded.

It was just on midnight as their car drove into Scotland Yard.

'Well I've had more than enough for one day, Andy, and I'm off home to dream about this frustrating case. It seems to me that everyone's behaving extremely suspiciously; they all had the opportunity to kill and the only thing we miss all along the line is motive. I shall probably have you arrested first thing in the morning. Meanwhile, good night.'

By the time Manton got home and into bed, he felt dog tired and as so often happens wide awake. As he lay in bed staring at the dark shape of the ceiling, his thoughts revolved around his mind and slowly, as drowsiness came over him, the chief characters danced before his eyes wearing masks of each other's faces, while he stood hypnotized and unable to move. Mr. Pinty's face grinned and bobbed about before him and suddenly the mask was removed and the dour expression of Inspector MacBruce took its place. The face of Miss Fenwick-Blunt wobbled like a jelly on a stick and just as Manton concluded she was dead, she peeled off the skin to reveal the white and frightened face of Albert Glindy. Gradually the horrible faces faded and he fell into a deep sleep.

Chapter Twenty-one

MORNING came almost before he felt he had got into bed. While he was shaving and his wife was cooking the breakfast and his small son, sitting on the bathroom chair, was plying him with questions about supersonic inter-planetary travel the telephone rang. Manton scraped off the last bit of soap from the left side of his chin and shouted down the stairs: 'O.K., Marjorie, I'll go.'

Two leaps brought him to the hall drying his face as he went. He lifted the receiver and immediately heard the voice of Sergeant Talper the other end. It was an excited and cheerful voice.

'Maisie Jenks and Hartman have been found.'

Manton grinned into the receiver.

'Fine, fine, now we really may become untangled and get ourselves somewhere. Where are they?'

'They were found living under an assumed name down Dartford way. It was their bad luck to take a room with a local constable's mother, and the latter became rather interested in her new lodgers and mentioned them to her son, and it didn't take him long to realize that there was something funny about the set-up.'

'Where are they now, Andy?'

'On their way up to the Yard, where they'll await your pleasure', replied Sergeant Talper breezily.

'Well they won't have to wait long. I'll just grab some breakfast and be on my way. See you anon.'

Manton replaced the receiver and dashed upstairs to complete his dressing and to submit himself for a few brief minutes to further inexorable questions on the habits of the latest jet fighter plane.

It was just before half-past nine when he arrived at his office and he was immediately informed that Jakes Hartman and his new wife were already in the building. Sergeant Talper, beaming all over his round face, entered the room while Manton was still taking off his overcoat.

'Seen them yet?' asked Manton.

'Just for a moment. They don't look as though they're exactly bursting with the joys of spring, but how much you'll get out of them is another matter.'

Manton nodded and said grimly: 'I'll find out just what made that girl scream if I have to turn her upside down and shake it out of her.'

Talper grinned. 'You may well have to do that.'

Simon Manton went round and sat behind his desk. 'Well there's no point in waiting, Andy, let's have the sacrificial victims led to the slaughter without delay.'

Talper left the room and Manton doodled abstractedly on the blotter, though his mind was working overtime.

It was about three minutes before the door opened again and the unwilling visitors were ushered in, followed by Sergeant Talper who quietly closed the door behind them. Manton greeted them.

'Good morning, Mr. and Mrs. Hartman', and there was a note of irony in his voice as he spoke. He motioned them to take chairs which Talper had brought forward, and was not slow to observe that while Jakes appeared to be drawn and nervous, the girl wore an expression of implacable obstinacy. After a moment's pause, he spoke.

'I think perhaps it would be best if we had our talks separately, so perhaps you'd wait outside, Mrs. Hartman, while I have first word with your husband.'

Manton's tone was quiet and silky and he could see that the arrangement was not at all to the liking of either of them. It was with reluctance that Maisie got up and, as she turned to go out of the room, she gave her unhappy looking husband a look which said clearly: 'You know what to say; stick to that and they can't do anything to you.' Talper led her out and across the corridor to a waiting-room. He then returned to the Inspector's office.

Jakes plucked nervously at the sides of his trousers and waited for the interview to begin. After giving him a little further time to grow even more uncomfortable, Manton cleared his throat.

'Well, Mr. Hartman, there are a good many points I want to ask you about, so we'd better start at the beginning. First of all, why did you leave your lodgings and do a moonlight flit?'

Jakes continued to look at the piece of floor between his feet when he answered.

'Because Maisie asked me to and I love her', he said in a dull unexpressive monotone.

The next question came immediately.

'What reason did she give for wanting you to run away with her like that?'

Jakes shifted uneasily on his hard chair. 'She was very upset by what had happened and wanted to get away from it all.'

'That's hardly an answer to my question', said Manton with quiet firmness. 'Why did she want to get away so dramatically and so completely from something in which she wasn't involved—or was she?' he added quietly.

Jakes looked up at his questioner. 'Good God, no!' he said showing some emotion for the first time since he'd entered the room.

'Why, then?' Manton's tone was relentless.

'I don't know—honestly I don't', said the other, now utterly miserable.

'Oh come now', said Manton firmly but pleasantly. 'You can hardly expect me to believe that.'

'It's the truth. I promise you it is. She arrived at my digs late the night of the murder and beseeched me to go away with her. I'd always loved her ever since I'd first seen her, and she was so pathetic and upset that evening that I was ready to do anything she asked me, even if it meant starting life completely anew.' He spoke rapidly with an undertone of bitterness in his voice, but Manton was not to be put off his course, and broke in again.

'That may account for why you left home that night, but it doesn't explain why you got married. Will you now answer me that one please?'

'I married her because I love her', and there was a note of defiance in his voice as Jakes spoke.

'An excellent reason to be sure. Now answer my question.'

'But honestly, Inspector. I'm telling you the truth.'

'You're telling me a series of half-truths and you're evading every question I ask you', said Manton. 'Perhaps you don't realize what a very awkward situation

145

you're in and what incalculable consequences may flow from this interview.'

Jakes blinked at him owlishly.

'Me in an awkward situation?' he asked, trying to sound surprised. 'I don't understand. What have I done?'

'At the most you've committed a murder. At the least you're an accessory after the fact to one', said Manton sternly.

For one moment it looked as if Jakes was going to fall off his chair, but he seemed to pull himself together, though it was a moment or so before his jaws joined company again.

'You can't really mean that, Inspector?'

'I can and do', said Manton without compromise. 'You don't think for a moment that I am not fully aware why you got married in such haste, do you?' he went on, and without waiting for an answer, which didn't seem forthcoming anyway, he pursued the hapless Jakes Hartman. 'It's quite clear that your wife screamed because she saw you just before you shot Tarrant. It may even be that it was pre-arranged that way. Afterwards you persuaded her to run away with you and get married because you know perfectly well that wives can't be made to give evidence against their husbands in capital charges. You can't sit in Court every day without picking up one or two bits of the law of evidence.'

Jakes was almost in tears but when Manton stopped speaking, he leapt from his chair and in choking tones shouted: 'Prove it! Prove it! I defy you to prove a single word. It's all a ghastly trick to try and make me incriminate myself.'

'We'll see', said Manton quietly. He turned to Talper. 'I think you might bring Mrs. Hartman now, Sergeant.'

Sergeant Talper got up and motioned to Jakes Hartman to follow him but Manton spoke again.

'Mr. Hartman needn't leave the room. Let him have a chair at the back there', and he indicated one against the wall behind the door. Jakes went to it and sat down and glowered out of the window as he slowly composed himself.

Mrs. Maisie Hartman *née* Jenks walked straight into the room and sat down. She crossed her legs and gazed steadily at Manton with a look of defiance in her eyes. She seemed unaware that her husband was also in the room, as he'd been partially hidden by the door when she entered and she had swept in like a '*grand dame*' without looking to left or right. She almost appeared to accept that he had disappeared through a trap door in the floor and been swallowed up in the dungeons below.

Manton met her gaze for some time before putting his first question.

'Why did your husband want you to run away with him?'

The answer was back almost before the question was asked.

'He didn't. It was the other way round.'

'Why did you ask him to run away and get married then?' asked Manton unruffled.

'I think that's my business', she replied briskly.

'You may think so; but it's also mine and I want an answer.'

She pursed her lips and that was all that Manton got by way of a reply. He frowned.

'Like your husband, I don't think you perhaps realize what a very serious position you're in, Mrs. Hartman', he said. 'I'm investigating a brutal murder; two brutal murders in fact, and I intend to get at the truth. If anyone obstructs me in that pursuit, they have to be dealt with. Now there are a number of points which I know you can assist me on, and let me say quite definitely so that you're under no misapprehension about it, I intend to have your assistance one way or another.' He paused and then said in a rather more gentle tone: 'If you go on like this, you'll only be butting your head against a stone wall and it'll get jolly sore in the process. And it won't get you any place, either.'

Maisie Hartman listened to this little speech but appeared to be quite unimpressed by it. However, Manton started his questioning again.

'What made you scream in Court just before Tarrant was killed? You obviously saw something and I want to know what it was.'

She looked up at Manton and then shifted her gaze to the window before bringing it back to him again. She appeared to be thinking with deep intensity before giving any reply to this very pertinent question.

'Why did you scream?' prompted Manton. Finally she seemed to make up her mind, and when she spoke her voice was level and quite composed.

'I screamed because I saw something; or rather thought I saw someone about to shoot. That was why I screamed.' An oppressive silence followed and then Manton spoke quietly again.

'You've only omitted one small detail. Who was it you saw about to shoot?'

'My husband,' she replied in an even tone and then went on, 'but of course I now realize how completely mistaken I was. It was the juror, Pinty, wasn't it? He first killed Tarrant and then himself.'

She looked white and tense as she spoke and behind her, sitting against the wall, was Jakes Hartman who stared blankly out of the window as though he'd not heard a word she'd said.

Another silence seemed to engulf all the four occupants of the room and it was Manton who finally broke it. 'And if that is so, why did you find it necessary to get married in such haste?' he asked disbelievingly.

'We'd always intended getting married sometime, and after we'd gone off and I'd discovered how wrong I was about it all; I mean about having thought it was Jakes I saw with the gun in his hand, we thought we might as well get married then and there, as we'd behaved pretty hastily already.'

'And what about the false name under which you were living until late last night? Why was that necessary if you'd discovered how wrong you were?' Manton asked. Maisie Hartman for a moment looked as though she were going to smile and anyway appeared relieved beyond measure to have got the interview through the storm and into the quiet waters the other side. Tenseness and truculence were fast draining out of her and being replaced by calm self-assurance.

'I'm afraid we rather lost our heads, and I suggested we'd best remain out of the way until the whole thing was cleared up and you'd made an arrest.'

'I suppose it never occurred to you,' said Manton quietly, 'that I couldn't make an arrest until you were found.'

'I tell you, Jakes Hartman had nothing to do with it at all', she said vehemently. 'How many more times do I have to repeat that I screamed because my mind played a trick on me and I thought it was he who had the revolver in his hand? I know now that I was utterly wrong and that's all there is to it.'

Manton nodded and then said: 'It really surprises me that a young woman of your obvious intelligence can first of all tell such a completely unconvincing story and in the second place expect even a stupid policeman to accept it.'

Their eyes met as he spoke and then the girl turned away and gave a petulant shrug of her shoulders. Manton appeared to be lost in deep thought for a moment or two but then his mind returned to the matter in hand and he rose from his chair.

'Well that'll be all for the moment but I shall want you to leave me an address where I can get hold of you at short notice and to promise not to leave it for any length of time without notifying me first.' As an afterthought he added: 'I suggest you go to your father's home, Mrs. Hartman.'

Maisie, who had also got up from her chair while he was speaking, switched round as he said this.

'We'll let you know where we are, I promise you that, Inspector Manton,' she said evenly, 'but there are certain reasons which make it impossible for us to go to my home.'

With that, she and her husband who still appeared to be in a daze, left the room, followed by Sergeant Talper.

'Come back when you've seen them out', Manton called out, as he closed the door behind them.

Alone in his room, Manton went over to the window and looked out at the buses which dead-marched, nose to tail, along the Embankment. He hummed a little tune to himself and was in good spirits in spite of the not very satisfactory course the recent interviews had followed. 'Wonder just what it is she's hiding,' he murmured to himself, 'but somehow I don't think it'll be very long now before we find out.'

The door opened and Sergeant Talper came back into the room.

'Well, Andy, do you think we're any further forward?' said Manton cheerfully.

Talper looked surprised at the other's tone.

'It seems to me they're all as guilty as each other', he said disgustedly. 'I suggest we put all their names in a hat and pick out the murderer. That girl's a cunning little so-and-so, and what she needs is a jolly good smack on her backside.'

Manton beamed happily at Sergeant Talper's indignation.

'I don't think it was as bad as all that.'

'You mean you think we've taken a step forward', said Talper, even more surprised.

'I've got a hunch, Andy, and I'm going to see if it'll work out. Meanwhile I want a complete check made on who Tarrant was consorting with before P.C. Moss was killed. More and more do I feel that the answer to the whole problem lies back as far as that.'

He opened the drawer at the side of his desk and pulled out the report which he'd received from the laboratory following the examination of Pinty's belongings. Sergeant Talper stood beside him and gazed moodily at it over his shoulder.

'Don't know what those lads get paid for', he said gloomily. 'All they do is mix pretty colours, boil them together, and look at the result through a microscope. And then all they tell you at the end is that nothing of any significance was found.' Manton laughed.

'You sound too frustrated for words. Those lab boys know their stuff. If there'd been anything of importance found about Pinty's clothing, they'd have found it and told us quickly enough.'

But Talper was not to be won over so easily.

'Just look at this for example: "*Handkerchief*—unsoiled and freshly laundered".'

'Well what's wrong with that?'

'Didn't everyone tell us he had a streaming cold and that his handkerchief was soaked in eucalyptus, and that he kept on holding it up to his nose. "Unsoiled and freshly laundered"—Can you beat it?'

Manton frowned.

'Yes, now you mention it, that's right. I wonder what happened to that handkerchief. It certainly wasn't with the things on the body.'

He put out his hand to the telephone, hesitated and drew it back. 'No—I think we'll go and see for ourselves.'

When they reached the laboratory they found their quarry bending intently over a microscope.

'Sorry to bother you, sir,' said Manton, 'but there's one point about Pinty's death that I'd like to check up on.'

'That being?'

'Have you got the handkerchief which was found with the body? I'd like to have a look at it for a moment.'

'Yes, I'll get it for you. It's in the locker with the rest of his things.'

The scientist left the two officers and returned shortly with a white handkerchief in his hand. Manton took it and put it up to his nose and sniffed.

'What's bothering you?'

'Only this; that we've been told that on the morning of Tarrant's murder and Pinty's disappearance, Pinty had a bad cold and his handkerchief reeked of eucalyptus. There's certainly not a trace of any on this one and I know from your report that you didn't find any.'

The scientist took the handkerchief from Manton and looked at it carefully. 'No, it scarcely needed scientific tests to tell us that it was unsoiled and quite clean. What is more we found no trace of eucalyptus on any of his clothing.'

There was a moment's thoughtful silence and then Manton spoke.

'Well that seems to be that. Thanks all the same, sir. We won't keep you any longer.'

The two men left the laboratory and returned to Manton's office. As they walked along the corridor, Manton murmured to himself: 'Very odd indeed. Now why should Pinty have got rid of his handkerchief after the murder of Tarrant and before his own death?'

'And his spectacles too', said Talper, as they entered the room.

'And his spectacles', repeated Manton staring furiously at the opposite wall. 'Handkerchief and spectacles. Why those two things above all others? Why those two at all?' he went on meditatively. Suddenly he leapt from his chair. 'Great heavens, yes! I see it now.

153

Of course it must have been that way. I've been blind, ever so blind, Andy. Now I know that my hunch is worth playing.'

With that he shot out of the room leaving the bewildered Talper wondering what it was all about.

Chapter Twenty-two

THE next two days Manton spent almost entirely in his room at Scotland Yard, going over and over again through every known detail of the two murders. He had now finally rejected the suicide theory in respect of the Pinty case and was working on the basis that both murders had been committed by the same person and furthermore that if that person felt him or herself to be in jeopardy, there might well be a third murder. Miss Fenwick-Blunt's experience proved that.

Sergeant Talper and other junior officers spent their time feeding Manton with the details he required, and it was noticeable that his appearance of cool confidence increased each time they brought him some fresh piece of information.

It was the early afternoon, and Sergeant Talper entered the room.

'The War Office have been checking the number of the revolver with which Pinty was shot. It seems that it was one that was on charge to the Three Hundred and Fifty-Third Regiment of Artillery and that it disappeared from that Unit in July forty-five. A Court of Inquiry was held but the missing weapon was never found. Presumably it's been through a good many hands since then.'

Manton's reply caused him to stare in complete stupefaction.

'If it's possible, Andy, I'd like to see a nominal roll of

all the officers and N.C.O.'s of that unit at the time the revolver disappeared.'

Talper continued to blink with surprise.

'Are you expecting to find that Miss Fenwick-Blunt was a Brigadier in the A.T.S. there or something?' he said as he left the room.

Manton laughed and returned his attention to the pile of papers before him. Eventually he put them on one side, put a sheet of clean foolscap paper in front of him in their place, and picked up a fresh, newly sharpened pencil and went into a session with himself.

Then he sat back in his chair and let his thoughts flow freely through his head. They went as follows: Whoever killed Tarrant, did so in sheer desperation. To have taken the risk which the killer took indicated that it was a question of then or never. That being so, what was the urgency? Clearly to prevent Tarrant saying something in evidence in open Court which would be disastrous for the killer. So disastrous in fact as to warrant an incredibly daring murder. But if it was Pinty who murdered Tarrant and then fled, how came he, himself, to meet his death? Having succeeded in his object, there would seem to be no point in his then killing himself. If he didn't, then someone else did, and who more likely than the murderer of Tarrant, who would have known immediately after by Pinty's conduct that another murder would be necessary if his identity was not to be revealed. If Pinty didn't commit suicide but was murdered, it was unlikely that he was killed by some friend of Tarrant's out of revenge. That being so, Pinty is ruled out as the murderer because (to summarize) if he killed Tarrant, then no object in committing suicide, and revenge by a friend of Tarrant is not a tenable theory. Who then could have murdered Tarrant and then Pinty? MacBruce had the opportunity and the motive. Glindy and Miss Fenwick-Blunt both had the opportunity and may also have had a motive. Hartman had the opportunity and maybe a motive too. Anyone of those four could have killed Tarrant in Court and then followed Pinty and disposed of him as well. None of them has got an unbreakable alibi as far as Pinty is concerned, largely because we can't be absolutely certain of the exact time he met his death. The doctor's evidence is that it might have been anything within four or five hours of the time when Tarrant was shot in Court. MacBruce and Hartman would certainly have had no difficulty in finding out where Pinty lived from the official Court record of jurors' addresses. Miss Blunt probably also knew by the second day of the trial. Now, taking the established facts and applying the possible theories, what's the answer? The answer is that I was right in playing my hunch and by to-morrow maybe we shall have somebody under arrest for double murder.

Manton emerged from his thoughts and leant forward to lift the telephone receiver from its cradle. He gave an extension number and a moment later said: 'Ask Sergeant Talper to come to my room, would you, please?'

When Talper came in, he looked at Manton with an obvious question-mark on his face.

'I think I've now got this straight, in my own head at least', said Manton. 'What is more I think the most effective way to wrap up this case and tie a neat bow around it, would be for us to stage what in German police procedure they call a confrontation. That is, we

157

have along all the chief actors in the drama and tell them a little story and watch their faces. It can often be most enlightening, Andy. So will you send out the necessary invitations for eleven o'clock to-morrow morning and we'll hope that nobody has any prior engagements.' He spoke light-heartedly and gave Talper a bland smile when the other continued standing there in hopeful silence. 'Don't look so shattered, it'll all turn out right in the end. Though there is one thing,' he went on seriously, 'I wouldn't like any of our guests to come to our party armed.'

Chapter Twenty-three

As Big Ben struck eleven the following morning, nine people sat tensely waiting in Detective Chief Inspector Manton's room. As the last echo of the great clock died away, Manton gazed round the assembly and appeared satisfied with what he saw.

The chairs were arranged in a semi-circle round his desk. On the far left of the circle as he looked at them sat Jakes and Maisie Hartman. The former still looked supremely unhappy and his spirits were obviously at their lowest ebb. His wife was dressed in the same dress she'd worn the day before, with a loose fitting tweed overcoat over it and no hat. She too was obviously living very much on her nerves and there were the beginnings of dark rings beneath her eyes, but for all that she still managed to look thoroughly feminine and attractive, though defiance and apprehension shone through her eyes. On her left sat Albert Glindy with his face looking whiter and more pointed than ever. He stared straight over Manton's head without shifting his gaze at all. Next to him was Inspector MacBruce looking severe and disapproving. On his other side sat Miss Fenwick-Blunt. She alone appeared to be quite enjoying the meeting and her lorgnettes were in constant use as she studied her fellow guests. Like Madame Defarge, she waited expectantly for the heads to roll, apparently unbothered by the possibility that her own might be amongst them. She wore the same green outfit and Manton concluded that she never appeared in public in anything else. She seemed quite to have recovered from her alarming experience of two nights before. On the far right of the circle sat Mr. Jenks, and Manton had noted his efforts to attract his daughter's attention and her equal determination not to look at him. It seemed probable that she had made no contact with her father since returning from out of the blue at Dartford. Sergeant Talper sat beside Manton on his right and on the other side sat young Detective Farley.

With the possible exception of Miss Fenwick-Blunt, Manton was obviously the only person in the room who was at his ease. Even Sergeant Talper fidgeted and kept rubbing the palms of his hands over his knee caps. Great though his loyalty was and considerable his faith in Manton, he had manifestly not liked the idea of this confrontation, as Manton had called it, from the very start. He was suspicious of all things unorthodox and never more so than when police methods were involved. He had not actually tried to dissuade Manton from the idea but he had hung back and denied it his enthusiasm. Now he sat rather like a small boy in the headmaster's study wondering just which of several disagreeable things was going to happen.

Manton surveyed the group and was conscious of the tension in the room. He had no desire to relieve it and, be the truth known, his whole aim was to maintain it at concert pitch. In staged effects like this one, no one knew better than he how essential it was for one person, and one alone, to retain the whip hand and call the tune, and that could only be accomplished where that person was able to increase or decrease the tension at will.

Manton looked about him with the calm assurance

of a chairman about to address a meeting of nervous shareholders who were trying to brace themselves for the worst. He cleared his throat and to his audience it was a portentous moment.

'Ladies and gentlemen,' he began, 'I asked you all to come along this morning to assist me in my investigation of this difficult case.' He paused but the eyes of his audience remained fixed upon him, and Miss Fenwick-Blunt adjusted her lorgnette for the better inspection of police officers. 'Though the facts of the case, or should I say cases, are mostly known to all of us here, I hope you'll forgive me if I briefly go over them again. Then they'll be clear in all our minds when we come to the later stage of this little meeting.'

Another pause and the mesmeric effect continued, and even good solid Sergeant Talper felt a tingling down his spine as he listened as intently as the others.

'On 8 November, the trial of William Edgar Tarrant opened before Mr. Justice Blaney in Number One Court at the Central Criminal Court. Tarrant was charged with the murder of a Police Constable Moss who'd been callously shot down while doing his duty. There was another man with Tarrant at the time, who in law was as guilty of murder as Tarrant; and it may even have been that it was this other man who actually fired the shot that killed the constable. The trial lasted the whole of one day but it came to an abrupt and dramatic finish early on the second when Tarrant himself was shot on the threshold of the witness box.' Manton surveyed the semi-circle of tense faces before him before going on: 'All you ladies and gentlemen were present in Court throughout the trial and at its untimely conclusion.'

161

He turned to Maisie Hartman at the extreme left. 'You, Mrs. Hartman, were sitting in the seats behind Counsel. You attended with your father as an interested spectator and got into Court through the good offices of your friend Mr. Jakes Hartman, who has since become your husband. Shortly before Tarrant was killed, you screamed. And if I may say so, there's seldom been a more effective or devastating scream. You, Mr. Hartman, were the official shorthand writer in Court at the time.' Here Manton switched his gaze to Jakes Hartman. 'When Tarrant was killed, he was within touching distance of yourself and Inspector MacBruce. Your small desk lies under the lee of the witness box and the narrow steps which lead to the latter pass between your desk and the Court Inspector's seat. Examination has revealed that Tarrant was shot at very close range—not that there was ever any doubt about that—and after the murder you suddenly left your abode and disappeared. And when you reappeared you had a wife.' Jakes Hartman gulped, and would have blushed as well if any increase of colour in his face could have been achieved.

Without waiting for any comment, Manton went on, next turning this attention to Glindy. 'You, Albert Glindy, are a warder at Brixton Prison and during the Tarrant trial you were doing escort duty at the Court. In fact you were escorting Tarrant to the witness box and were only a pace behind him when he was murdered. You had come to know Tarrant in the prison and had been in quite close contact with him for some time.' As the Inspector spoke, the warder's skin looked as though it might suddenly rip across his cheekbones, so taut did it appear. 'Immediately after the murder you, Glindy, vanished from the scene and according to yourself, you went down below to be sick. At all events you left the man you were meant to be guarding in the oddest circumstances and at the very moment that he needed attention.' Manton stared coolly at the warder for a full thirty seconds before meeting with his own, the sullen smouldering gaze of Inspector Robert MacBruce. 'As I've already said, Inspector MacBruce was the uniformed Court Inspector at the time and his official seat, as by now you all know, is that small cubby hole just beneath the foreman of the jury and on one side of the steps that lead up to the witness box. All along, Inspector MacBruce has shown ill-concealed impatience at the manner in which I have conducted my investigation and a marked disinclination to assist me as behoves one policeman to another. Of course, it was only later that I learned that the Inspector and the murdered man had become acquainted some years ago and that their acquaintanceship had, from the Inspector's point of view, a most unhappy result.' Here Manton paused, and stared evenly at the man about whom he was speaking, who for his part showed no emotion beyond a hardening look of the eyes and a slight twitch at the corner of his mouth.

Next Manton turned to Miss Fenwick-Blunt who had her lorgnette up and was ready for the attack. 'Miss Fenwick-Blunt, as she is now called, was a juror in the Tarrant trial and she sat just behind the foreman, so that she too was quite close to Tarrant when he was killed and she had as good an opportunity as any to commit the murder. In fact, always supposing that even though Tarrant turned his head at that devastating scream but did not turn his body as well, the path of the bullet makes it certain that either one of two people was the murderer—and you, Miss Fenwick-Blunt, are one of them.'

As Manton had finished with one person, so all eyes had generally turned to the next, but on this occasion that formidable woman found herself the continuing subject of interest of everyone in the room. She however, continued to gaze straight at Manton and appeared undisturbed and unruffled by his insinuations.

'You, Mr. Jenks,' went on Manton, 'were there as an interested spectator and sat, as I've already mentioned, with your daughter in the City Lands seats beneath the public gallery and behind Counsel. Your daughter's disappearance soon after the murder appeared to cause you genuine surprise and anxiety, and it is quite clear that the murder could not have been committed from where you and your daughter were sitting.' Manton surveyed the whole group again before continuing: 'That deals with the position in Court at the time of the murder of all of you who are present in this room to-day. You have each one of you at one or more times in the history of the case behaved with great stupidity and have even lied to the police, which, in an investigation of this kind, is a very serious thing to do. Why you so acted, we shall see in due course. But for all that, only one amongst you is a murderer.'

The silence which followed this last observation was as profound as it was ominous. Not one of his audience seemed able to take his or her eyes off Manton and their very lives might have depended on the intensity of the looks that bored into him.

He, for his part, seemed quite unaffected by them

and, on the contrary, to be luxuriating in his oracular rôle.

'Some murders,' he went on unhurriedly, 'can be solved by a study of the method by which they are committed; others by finding the motive; but all of them involve a mass of detailed, painstaking and routine detection work.' He might have been lecturing young detectives at Hendon on 'The Investigation of Crime' rather than addressing a small bunch of taut-nerved people, one of whom was a diabolically clever murderer. 'From the first moment of this case it has been clear to my colleagues and myself that motive was the all important feature. *Cherchez la* motive has been our slogan all the time. Once it was found, then everything was likely to become clear and the most baffling aspects of the case would resolve themselves and stand out in stark relief against the obvious. So long as we failed to discover, or should I say uncover, the motive for these murders, then we were only going round in circles, and however many bits of the puzzle we were able to put together, the pattern was always blurred and unintelligible without the motive being added. The trouble has been that several of you had motives to kill Tarrant, and that, in some measure, explains your subsequent conduct which I have already stigmatized as extremely stupid.'

The interruption which followed, was as sudden as it was unexpected.

'For God's sake stop this cat and mouse game.' Albert Glindy started from his chair as he shouted at the surprised Manton. 'If you think one of us has committed a murder, accuse him. Accuse me if you bloody well want to, but get on with it.' After this outburst he

165

sank back on to his chair, trembling violently from head to foot.

'You'd better fetch him a glass of water', said Manton calmly to the young officer next to him. The latter got up and left the room to return a moment later bearing a cracked tea-cup with water in it. This was handed to Glindy who took it as a matter of course and gulped it down. Complete silence reigned during the enactment of this little piece of by-play. Whatever the rest of Manton's audience had felt about it, none of them had elected to give public support to the warder's charge.

When Manton spoke again it was as if nothing untoward had happened at all.

'I was about to enlarge on the question of motive. As I said before, it provides the complete answer to this case and I must confess it hasn't been an easy task to uncover the motive.' Looking at Jakes Hartman, he went on: 'It took me a long time to find out what motive you might have for killing Tarrant, but it was quite obvious that somewhere there must be one, for otherwise your subsequent conduct was inexplicable. You knew that Tarrant had at one time pestered your wife with his attentions and that if, as appeared possible, he were acquitted, he might attempt to renew his associations with her and so you decided not to risk his being set at large again and you shot him dead in Court. In fact, a mixture of jealousy and prevention being better than cure attitude prompted you to act as you did.'

At this point three people spoke at once. The hapless Jakes, frightened but defiant, said in a far from confident voice: 'It's all lies and you can't prove a single word of it.'

His wife who was on her feet, gave Manton a withering look as she spoke. 'You've no right to make such wicked allegations when you know that they aren't true. You've no authority to keep us here and I really see no reason why we should stay while you stage your silly little jokes.'

The third member of the audience who was roused into speech by the Inspector's attack on his new son-in-law was Mr. Jenks.

'How dare you suggest that my daughter has been flirting with a murderer', he said in quiet but angry tones.

Manton smiled in his direction.

'In the first place I didn't say she'd flirted with him, and in the second he wasn't a murderer then, even if he subsequently became one.'

Mr. Jenks made an unspellable noise and turning to the two newly-weds Manton went on: 'I think it would be better if you stayed till the end.' And it was obvious that he meant it. 'Let me remind you that at the moment I'm only considering the various motives which you severally had for committing this murder. I'm not yet making any actual charges.'

'Because you obviously can't', snorted the hitherto silent MacBruce.

Manton ignored the further interruption and went on determinedly: 'As far as Mrs. Hartman is concerned, motive doesn't enter into it as it's clear that she couldn't have murdered Tarrant from where she was. But it would very much appear to be the case that she saw Mr. Hartman about to fire the pistol and that this caused her to scream and faint. Later it had the further effect of causing her to become Mrs. Hartman, thereby legally bottling herself up as a potential witness—in fact as the only eye-witness of what happened.'

Manton surveyed the group again before resting his gaze on Albert Glindy.

'You saw a good deal of Tarrant in prison before his trial and at the Court in the course of it. Shall we say that your relationship with him was not exactly in accordance with prison regulations and that had the Governor learned of some of the little services you performed for one of his charges, he might have shown a certain disapproval which might have gone so far as to cost you your job.' Glindy appeared to be about to start out of his chair again, but Manton went on quickly: 'Just a minute, let me finish before you make wild protests. I have made fairly careful inquiries at the prison and I'm quite satisfied that you were in fact trafficking things in and out for Tarrant while he was there. What then was easier than for him to increase his demands on your services, knowing, as he did, that once you'd helped him there was no turning back. And supposing you did demur and try to refuse, it was so simple for him to bring you to your senses again. A person awaiting trial for murder is in many ways a pampered creature and it only needed a word from Tarrant for your indiscretions to be laid bare and your job lost.' Manton paused and then added significantly: 'And men at your age can't afford to lose their jobs and their pension rights. And after all, you might rightly reason that you were only anticipating the hangman by a week or two.'

Miss Fenwick-Blunt nodded interestedly as Manton voiced this view.

'I always thought it was him all along', she said pleasantly.

Glindy himself appeared to be transfixed and incapable of reaction. He just sat very white-faced and with small beads of perspiration breaking out on his forehead and at his temples.

'But what about the note you found on Pinty's body?' broke in MacBruce.

Manton nodded keenly.

'Exactly. Who was in a better position to plant that letter on Pinty's corpse than Glindy. He first shot Tarrant for reasons which I've indicated. Pinty saw him do it and dashed out of Court. You may remember that, as he fled, Pinty told the Judges' usher that he saw the murderer and that the latter pointed the pistol at him afterwards, and that was why he didn't wait to see what happened next. Glindy then had to silence Pinty. He successfully accomplished this and knowing that we strongly suspected Pinty, at that time, of being Tarrant's murderer, what was easier for him than to consolidate his position by planting a fake note on Pinty's body which purported to come from Tarrant and appeared in somewhat mysterious terms to give Pinty a motive for having murdered Tarrant. And I must confess that we swallowed it hook, line and sinker.'

Manton had been addressing his remarks to MacBruce and virtually ignored the subject of them, who sat slumped in his chair. 'There's a further point. Who better than Glindy was able to get hold of the special paper which is supplied to prisoners for writing their letters?'

At this, Glindy sprang from his chair and turning

towards Miss Fenwick-Blunt shouted at her in a wildly hysterical voice: 'This is all your doing, you bloody old bitch.'

Before anyone had time to react to this outburst, he had plunged across the room and the door was slamming behind him.

Chapter Twenty-four

THE meeting had broken up shortly after Glindy's departure, and Manton was alone in his room with Sergeant Talper.

'It didn't quite work out as you expected, did it, sir?' asked the latter doubtfully.

'Not exactly.'

Manton was thoughtful as he spoke and didn't appear as much discouraged by events as Talper had expected him to be. When Glindy had made his sudden dramatic departure, Sergeant Talper had been all prepared for Manton to chase after him down the passage and bring him back with a murder charge tied round his neck. Not only had Manton not done this but he hadn't even lifted the telephone receiver to have him stopped at the main entrance. In fact he'd brought the meeting to a close in quite a matter of fact fashion as though nothing untoward had happened.

There was a knock on the door and Detective Farley came in. 'Excuse me, sir,' he began, 'but that woman is back and wants to have a word with you.'

'What woman are you talking about?' asked Manton.

'That Miss Fenwick-Blunt.'

Manton looked up sharply.

'Well, well, I wonder what she wants now . . . I suppose you had better show her in.'

The two officers remained silent and thoughtful as they waited for their visitor to arrive. A few moments later there was a knock on the door again and Miss

Fenwick-Blunt sailed in with all the self-assurance of a Member of Parliament about to address his rustic constituents.

'I felt I simply had to come back, Inspector. I was so enjoying our little meeting when it came to its sudden end. I realize, of course, that you've now caught the murderer, but I was so looking forward to hearing what you were going to say about me when my turn came to be put on a slide under your microscope.'

She spoke confidently and one might almost say brazenly. So much so that when she ceased talking, Manton couldn't bring himself to say anything in reply for some moments and could only sit and marvel at her supreme composure.

You really are a remarkable woman, he thought to himself. Aloud he said : 'Seeing that you've returned to the spider's parlour of your own free will, I think perhaps I'll ask you some questions first.' She waited expectantly and again in no way appeared put out by the underlying note of menace in Manton's voice. 'You may recall that you visited Scotland Yard and saw me in this room on the evening of the Tarrant murder. You said you had come along to help me and mentioned quite casually and gratuitously that you'd been spending the previous few hours in a cinema.' Here he paused and fixed her with a steady stare. 'I've since discovered that that was not true and that in fact you paid a visit to south London that evening. Would you now care to tell me why you told me a lie and went out of your way to do so, and secondly what business you had in Brixton that made it necessary to lie?'

A silence followed. Simon Manton stared hard at her and she in turn riveted her gaze a few inches over the top of his head. Sergeant Talper looked from one to the other as if fully expecting to see either of them vanish in a puff of smoke.

'As you don't seem too keen to answer my questions,' Manton went on after a pause, 'may I suggest the truth to you in the form of another question? Am I not right in thinking that you went all the way to Brixton on that cold November evening to visit our friend of this morning who brought the meeting to such a sudden close— to visit Albert Glindy, in fact?' Miss Fenwick-Blunt still remained silent and outwardly in full control of her emotions. 'You see, madam, I now happen to know that you are comparatively experienced in the ways and customs of our criminal courts and that the inside of prison walls are not unknown to you.'

There was still no response and Manton went on almost with relish it seemed. 'Once a blackmailer, always a blackmailer. They're ever on the look-out for new possibilities of exploitation. You saw such a possibility in the conduct of Albert Glindy. No doubt you observed that little incident when Tarrant came into dock on the morning of his death and put Glindy very much in his place when the latter was trying to hurry him along. You realized at once that Tarrant had some hold over him or something of the sort, and you wasted not a minute in dashing off that evening to put your ideas to the test. I'm right, aren't I?'

It seemed an age before Miss Fenwick-Blunt lowered her gaze and met Manton's eyes with hers.

'Of course, Inspector, I must admit to having been in prison as that's all amongst your records. But it was a long while ago and since then Miss Fenwick-Blunt has never been in trouble. Jane Webber lies buried within the precincts of the prison, like an executed murderer. It was Victoria Fenwick-Blunt who stepped through the heavy gates that early summer morning twelve years ago.'

'But am I right about your visiting Glindy?'

'In view of the fact that I believe I have the honour to be one of your suspects still, I think I'd prefer not to discuss this matter any further.'

Manton smiled.

'You forget that it was you who paid me this visit. I didn't ask you to come. I agree that your position is not an enviable one because anyone who behaves in a murder case as you have done is in deadly peril of finding their way to prison—back to prison, should I say.'

Miss Fenwick-Blunt got up and looking quite expressionless turned her back on the two officers and left the room.

'The way our guests walk out on us', murmured Manton as he watched the door close behind her.

'Do you really think she tried to blackmail Glindy?' asked Talper.

'I'm certain of it, Andy. All the way through this case, she has endeavoured by various subtle means to convey to our minds that he was involved. And I believe, if the truth be known, that she was doing this as part of a cold, deliberate plan to squeeze money out of him. You know, "you pay me or I'll say you did it" sort of business. She even described the man who, she says, attempted to murder her in the image of Glindy.'

'You don't think that was genuine then?'

'I'm darned certain it wasn't and have been certain for a very long time. I think it was deliberately and cunningly staged in order to direct our minds further towards Glindy. And if he'd succumbed to her villainous blackmail, I don't doubt she'd have then back-pedalled a bit and suggested in some way that it couldn't have been Glindy after all or at least that it was less likely to have been him.'

'Why don't we pull her in?' asked Talper who'd reached the stage of asking questions.

'One thing no evidence, and secondly, there's time enough. Let's get our murderer under lock and key first.' Manton paused and looked thoughtful. 'And I don't think it'll be very long before we do that.' He smiled at Talper and went on: 'I know you don't like my parties with our suspects, but I'm going to get them all along to the Old Bailey to-morrow morning. I'm still playing a hunch that we've almost got our murderer to sign his own execution warrant and to-morrow may see him do it.'

Chapter Twenty-five

OVERNIGHT the fog came down again and the following morning it lay over the city like a yellow pall. People hurrying to their work left their buses and got there quicker on foot, and those emerging from the underground coughed and groped their way along the crowded pavements. Everyone softly cursed the fog and his neighbour who suddenly barged into him and vanished again without an apology.

Detective Chief Inspector Manton and Detective Sergeant Talper arrived together at the Old Bailey and disappeared inside before one or two press men, who had got wind of what was going to take place, could see who they were. The building seemed almost deserted and its atmosphere was far from being a friendly one. The doorkeeper nodded to them as they went past and told Manton that three of his guests had already arrived and were waiting up in Number One Court. The officers ran up the stairs two at a time and pushed through the swing doors which led into the Court. Sitting just inside in one of the rows behind the dock were Maisie and Jakes Hartman and Inspector MacBruce.

'Good morning', said Manton. His greeting was briefly and unenthusiastically acknowledged. 'I expect the others will be here in a minute. They've probably got held up by the fog. It seems to be thicker than ever now. We haven't had such a bad one since the day that Tarrant was murdered.'

There was no response to this gratuitously provocative remark. The next twenty minutes were a tiresome wait for everyone but by the end of that time the others had all arrived. They sat together in one row and Manton stood with his back to the dock and addressed them.

'Now that we're all here—and I'm very much obliged to you for turning up on such a foul day—I want, with your assistance, to re-enact precisely what each one of you was doing when Mrs. Hartman let out her scream and what you did immediately after it. Would you now all please go and sit in the seats you were occupying when Tarrant was murdered.' Manton turned to Sergeant Talper. 'Sergeant would you please go and sit in the jury box where Pinty sat?'

With their footsteps echoing round the otherwise deserted Court, Manton's little group shuffled out of the row where they'd been sitting and took up their positions.

Manton himself went down to the big table in the well of the Court and cast an approving glance around him. Alone in the dock, and obviously feeling every bit as conspicuous as he looked, sat Albert Glindy, his gaze fastened steadfastly ahead. Miss Fenwick-Blunt, Sergeant Talper, Inspector MacBruce and Jakes Hartman sat, as before, close to the witness box, which now stood empty like a deserted and unwalled telephone kiosk. Up in the seats beneath the public gallery (the City Lands seats) were Harry Jenks and his daughter, and Manton noticed that Maisie sat aloof from her father with a small space between them. He went up to where they were and surveyed the scene again.

'Now when I give the signal, I want you, Glindy,

to leave the dock and make your way to the witness box and the rest of you to imagine that Tarrant is just a pace or two ahead of him.' He looked around to make sure that his instructions were being followed. 'When Glindy reaches the bottom of the steps by Inspector MacBruce I want you, Mrs. Hartman, to give us one of your best screams and you, Sergeant Talper, immediately to dash out through that door, by the witness box, run along the corridor behind the Judge's seat and come in by this one.' Manton pointed to the door through which those occupying the City Lands seats entered and left the Court.

'Everyone clear?'

They might have been clear but certainly none of them showed any enthusiasm for the idea. Maisie Hartman was the only one to speak, however.

'It's no good, Inspector, I simply can't go through all that again. And the idea of screaming in cold blood in this—' she paused and shuddered—'in this eerie atmosphere is just too horrible.'

'All right,' said Manton equably, 'I'll scream for you.' Maisie moved along and Manton sat down next to Mr. Jenks who was on the outside of the row.

'O.K. let's start', said Manton. Looking like a wax dummy and moving as if by clockwork, Glindy got up from his chair in the dock, walked to the door which led down into the Court, slid the catch and stepped out. Seven pairs of eyes watched him with an even greater intensity than they had Tarrant when he made the same journey on that fateful morning. To Jakes Hartman sitting behind his little table, it seemed an eternity before the warder reached the bottom of the steps which led up to the witness box.

If Maisie's original scream had been effective, Manton's now was doubly so, and lost nothing by being expected. Even Sergeant Talper was momentarily transfixed but then he shot from his seat and charged for the door. Manton meanwhile had flopped over and was lying across Harry Jenks' lap, but almost before he'd assumed the position, Sergeant Talper had re-entered the Court and was standing beside him on the steps which led down to the front rows used by Counsel and to the Clerk of the Court's desk.

Manton gazed very hard into Jenks' face and sniffed once or twice. Then slowly he raised himself from the embarrassed man's lap and stood up.

'Is that the same overcoat you were wearing when you attended the Tarrant trial?' he asked.

'I can't remember whether I wore an overcoat that day but this is the only one I've got.'

'Then perhaps you can explain why there's a faint odour of eucalyptus round the breast pocket.'

Jenks only paused a moment before answering. 'I always use it on my handkerchiefs when I have a cold and it's apt to cling for some time.'

'Exactly', said Manton. 'Harry Jenks I'm going to arrest you——' He got no further, as the next moment Jenks hurled himself past Sergeant Talper and was out of the Court.

Chapter Twenty-six

'I'LL start at the beginning', said Manton smoothly. Jenks had for the moment made good his escape but after giving the necessary instructions, the rest of the party had returned with Manton and Talper to Scotland Yard where they were now once more ensconced in Manton's room.

'As with so many cases, it was pure routine detective work which put me on the right trail in this one. Just after the end of the war one of many pistols on charge to the Three Hundred and Fifty-Third Regiment of Artillery disappeared, and though an Army Court of Inquiry was held, the weapon was never found and no one ever discovered what happened to it—that is not until the other day.' Manton paused for effect before going on: 'It was with that missing pistol that Pinty was shot; and it was that same weapon which was also used on 11 September to kill P.C. Moss, the crime of which Tarrant was accused.' Manton surveyed his audience and savoured their rapt attention. 'I must confess that I didn't expect to have success with my next step, but I checked the names of everyone who'd been serving with that regiment at the time when the pistol disappeared to see if I could find any direct link. As I say, I didn't expect to do so as it was more than probable that the weapon had passed through a good many hands before reaching those of the murderer. However, I was more than interested to find amongst the many names which I checked that of a Lance Bombardier

Ronald Jenks, and it didn't take me long to discover further that he is the son of Mr. Harry Jenks and the brother of Mrs. Hartman. My subsequent inquiries showed me that Ronald Jenks, like so many young men in the immediate post-war years, found it difficult to settle down. He craved for excitement. He was extravagant in his tastes and found his wages as a junior clerk in a firm of surveyors quite inadequate to his needs. He kept bad company, and being weak and lacking in moral fibre, he was easily led astray. The types he consorted with flattered his ego, satisfied his vanity and shaped him to their own infamous ends. And so the time came when he met William Edgar Tarrant.' Manton paused again and went on with dramatic suddenness. 'It was Ronald Jenks who was with Tarrant on the night when P.C. Moss was shot. I am convinced that it was he who in fact fired the fatal shot; it was completely out of keeping with Tarrant to carry firearms on any of his exploits. I believe that young Jenks lost his head, murdered Moss and made good his escape. I believe that on his return home that night—and he must have been in a pretty panicky state when he did get back there—he told his father exactly what had happened and placed himself completely under his orders.' Manton warmed to his subject. 'Harry Jenks at once realized that there was always a danger that Tarrant would implicate Ronald. It might happen at any moment. However, by the time the trial started, he apparently hadn't done so and the secret of that night remained between the three men; father, son and accused. No one realized better than Jenks senior that Tarrant might suddenly come out with the whole truth at his trial in a final endeavour to extricate himself.

And so he came along to Court and at the end of the first day he heard Tarrant say that he'd have to make certain disclosures when he gave his evidence, and he knew that the sands were running out against him. At ten-thirty the next morning, Tarrant would go into the witness box and tell all the world that his confederate on the night of the murder was Ronald Jenks. Jenks senior had very little time in which to act and his task was an almost superhuman one. How could Tarrant be silenced effectively and for all time between then and the next morning? A desperate situation is said to call for bold measures and it must certainly be conceded that the measure which he decided upon was as bold as it was brilliant in design and almost perfect in execution.'

No one spoke or stirred as Manton approached the climax of his story.

'There were two very curious and odd features about the Pinty murder and it's only quite recently that I've been able to fit them into their proper place. For a long time they puzzled me by their apparent incongruity. One was that Pinty's spectacles were never found on his body, although we knew he never went anywhere without them; and the other was that on the second day, Pinty had a bad cold and sniffed constantly into his handkerchief which was drenched with eucalyptus; yet when we found his body on Hampstead Heath, the only handkerchief was a clean one which had certainly not got any eucalyptus on it. As I say, I found these two features most perplexing. At first they didn't seem awfully important and yet all the time at the back of my mind, I felt that they had some hidden and even vital significance. Why, I kept on asking myself after I was certain that Pinty had been murdered and had not committed suicide, should anyone have removed his spectacles and handkerchief? And suddenly the answer came in a rush.'

The pause which followed was almost unbearable in its intensity. Nobody spoke, nobody moved, and the very tenseness in the air hurt. After what seemed to be an interminable time, Manton went on in the same even tone, a tone which belied the sensation of fluttering insects he had in his stomach.

'The answer was so simple that I nearly missed it. It was and it wasn't Pinty who shot Tarrant in Court that fatal morning.'

Sergeant Talper started with surprise.

'By half-past ten on the second morning of the trial, the unfortunate Mr. Pinty already lay dead on Hampstead Heath. Because, on his way to Court that foggy day, he was suddenly offered a lift, and little did he know when he accepted it, that the driver of the car had had him under almost unceasing observation since the previous evening, and had planned his death with minute care. And the man who took his place in the jury box that day, the man who wore his spectacles and had such a bad cold that he had to hold a handkerchief permanently up to his face was Harry Jenks, the father who was determined to protect his son and if necessary, commit murder to do so; or should I say to commit one cold-blooded murder in order that he might commit a second one. The first being merely a means to the second.'

'What about the note that was found on Pinty's body?' It was the first interruption there'd been since Manton started his story and it was Inspector MacBruce who asked the question.

'The note was genuine enough in one way,' said Manton, 'but its use by Jenks was a brilliant stroke. Tarrant sent that note to young Jenks from prison, and incidentally one must hand it to Tarrant that he gave his confederate every chance to go away and disappear before the truth came out. Well, to get back to the note which I don't doubt was smuggled out and posted.' Here he glanced at Glindy who studiously avoided his look. 'Young Jenks of course showed it to his father and he saw what a wonderful red herring it would prove to be if planted on Pinty's body, since the automatic assumption would be that it had been sent by Tarrant to Pinty. And furthermore, it appeared to provide Pinty with a motive for having murdered Tarrant.'

It was Miss Fenwick-Blunt's turn to ask a question.

'And may we be told why Mrs. Hartman let out that scream of hers?'

'I should have thought it was obvious', said Manton. 'She suddenly recognized her father through his disguise as he sat in Pinty's place on the jury. By the time she came round from her faint, he was beside her again having slipped back into Court, as Sergeant Talper did a short time ago, unnoticed in the general confusion and when all attention was riveted on where Tarrant's dead body lay. The reason no one saw him leave the building was because he never did and of course he removed Pinty's spectacles and the handkerchief as he raced round the Judge's corridor.' Manton turned to Maisie Hartman. 'That's a fair summary as far as you're concerned, isn't it?'

The girl looked pale and tense and just gave a slight nod in confirmation.

The following day Jenks was arrested on board a small foreign cargo steamer about an hour before she sailed from Cardiff docks and a few weeks later he found himself back in Number One Court at the Old Bailey occupying yet a different seat again; this time the central one in that dramatic building.

Before the trial Maisie and Jakes Hartman slipped quietly away to start life afresh in a new land.

On the day that Jenks was convicted and sentenced to death, Inspector MacBruce entered the kitchen of his home and tossed a revolver on to the table. His wife looked at it and then at her husband.

'I thought it as well not to have it about the place while that fool Manton was nosing around', he said. But MacBruce's opinion of Manton was shared neither by the public nor, more important perhaps, by his superiors.

'What about a nice juicy fraud next time, Andy?' asked Manton as they left the building. 'All figures and accounts and ten column schedules.'

'All right for some, sir, I've no doubt. But give me a nice bit of violence every time. It's far easier to follow a trail of blood than one of bank entries.'

They crossed the road and the doors of the 'Dying Duck' swung behind them.

THE END

〉〉〉 If you've enjoyed this book and would like to discover more great vintage crime and thriller titles, as well as the most exciting crime and thriller authors writing today, visit: 〉〉〉

The Murder Room
Where Criminal Minds Meet

themurderroom.com

www.ingramcontent.com/pod-product-compliance
Ingram Content Group UK Ltd.
Pitfield, Milton Keynes, MK11 3LW, UK
UKHW040436280225
455666UK00003B/98